...*And the Earth Did Not Devour Him*

and Related Readings

McDougal Littell
A HOUGHTON MIFFLIN COMPANY

Evanston, Illinois   Boston   Dallas

Acknowledgments

Arte Público Press: . . . *And the Earth Did Not Devour Him* by Tomás
Rivera, translated by Evangelina Vigil-Piñón. Copyright © 1987
by Concepción Rivera. Copyright of the Translation © 1987 by
Evangelina Vigil-Piñón. Reprinted with permission from the pub-
lisher, Arte Público Press, University of Houston.

Washington State University Press: Excerpt from *Fields of Toil:
A Migrant Family's Journey* by Isabel Valle. Copyright © 1994 by the
Board of Regents of Washington State University. Reprinted with
permission from Washington State University Press, Pullman,
Washington.

Bilingual Press/Editorial Bilingüe: "Latin Women Pray," from
Reaching for the Mainland and Selected New Poems by Judith Ortiz
Cofer. Copyright © 1995 by Bilingual Press/Editorial Bilingüe.
Reprinted by permission of Bilingual Press/Editorial Bilingüe,
Arizona State University, Tempe, Ariz.

Susan Bergholz Literary Services: "Napa, California," from *My
Father Was a Toltec* by Ana Castillo. Copyright © 1995 by Ana
Castillo. Reprinted by permission of Susan Bergholz Literary
Services, New York. All rights reserved.

Continued on page 165

Cover illustration by Michael Steirnagle.
Author photo: Arte Público Press.

ISBN 0-395-77139-0

Printed in China

9 10 11 12 DSC 09 08

Contents

...*And the Earth Did Not Devour Him*

Tomás Rivera

Translated by
Evangelina Vigil-Piñón

. . . And the Earth Did Not Devour Him

The Lost Year

〰️

That year was lost to him. At times he tried to remember and, just about when he thought everything was clearing up some, he would be at a loss for words. It almost always began with a dream in which he would suddenly awaken and then realize that he was really asleep. Then he wouldn't know whether what he was thinking had happened or not.

It always began when he would hear someone calling him by his name but when he turned his head to see who was calling, he would make a complete turn and there he would end up—in the same place. This was why he never could discover who was calling him nor why. And then he even forgot the name he had been called.

One time he stopped at mid-turn and fear suddenly set in. He realized that he had called himself. And thus the lost year began.

He tried to figure out when that time he had come to call "year" had started. He became aware that he was always thinking and thinking and from this there was no way out. Then he started thinking about how he never thought and this was when his mind would go blank and he would fall asleep. But before falling asleep he saw and heard many things . . .

What his mother never knew was that every night he would drink the glass of water that she left under the bed for the spirits. She always believed that they drank the water and so she continued doing her duty. Once he was going to tell her but then he thought that he'd wait and tell her when he was grown up.

The Children Couldn't Wait

The heat had set in with severity. This was unusual because it was only the beginning of April and this kind of heat was not expected until the end of the month. It was so hot that the bucket of water the boss brought them was not enough. He would come only two times for the midday and sometimes they couldn't hold out. That was why they took to drinking water from a tank at the edge of the furrow. The boss had it there for the cattle and when he caught them drinking water there he got angry. He didn't much like the idea of their losing time going to drink water because they weren't on contract, but by the hour. He told them that if he caught them there again he was going to fire them and not pay them. The children were the ones who couldn't wait.

"I'm very thirsty, Dad. Is the boss gonna be here soon?"

"I think so. You can't wait any longer?"

"Well, I don't know. My throat already feels real dry. Do you think he's almost gonna be here? Should I go to the tank?"

"No, wait just a little longer. You already heard what he said."

"I know, that he'll fire us if he catches us there, but I can't wait."

"Come on now, come on, work. He'll be here real soon."

"Well . . . I'll try to wait. Why doesn't this one let us bring water? Up north . . ."

"Because he's no good, that's why."

"But we could hide it under the seat, couldn't we? It was always better up north . . . And what if I make like I'm gonna go relieve myself by the tank?"

And this was what they started doing that afternoon. They pretended they were going to relieve themselves and they would go on to the edge of the tank. The boss became aware of this almost right away. But he didn't let on. He wanted to catch a bunch of them and that way he could pay fewer of them and only after they had done more work. He noticed that one of the children kept going to drink water every little while and he became more and more furious. He thought then of giving him a scare and he crawled on the ground to get his rifle.

What he set out to do and what he did were two different things. He shot at him once to scare him but when he pulled the trigger he saw the boy with a hole in his head. And the child didn't even jump like a deer does. He just stayed in the water like a dirty rag and the water began to turn bloody . . .

"They say that the old man almost went crazy."

"You think so?"

"Yes, he's already lost the ranch. He hit the bottle pretty hard. And then after they tried him and he got off free, they say he jumped off a tree 'cause he wanted to kill himself."

"But he didn't kill himself, did he?"

"Well, no."

"Well, there you have it."

"Well, I'll tell you, compadre, I think he did go crazy. You've seen the likes of him nowadays. He looks like a beggar."

"Sure, but that's 'cause he doesn't have any more money."

"Well . . . that's true."

She had fallen asleep right away and everyone, very mindful of not crossing their arms nor their legs nor their hands, watched her intensely. The spirit was already present in her body.

"Let's see, how may I help you this evening, brothers and sisters?"

"Well, you see, I haven't heard from my boy in two months. Yesterday a letter from the government arrived telling me that he's lost in action. I'd like to know whether or not he's alive. I feel like I'm losing my mind just thinking and thinking about it."

"Have no fear, sister. Julianito is fine. He's just fine. Don't worry about him anymore. Very soon he'll be in your arms. He'll be returning already next month."

"Thank you, thank you."

A Prayer

〰

Dear God, Jesus Christ, keeper of my soul. This is the third Sunday that I come to implore you, beg you, to give me word of my son. I have not heard from him. Protect him, my God, that no bullet may pierce his heart like it happened to Doña Virginia's son, may he rest in God's peace. Take care of him for me, Dear Jesus, save him from the gunfire, have pity on him who is so good. Since he was a baby, when I would nurse him to sleep, he was so gentle, very grateful, never biting me. He's very innocent, protect him, he does not wish to harm anyone, he is very noble, he is very kind, may no bullet pierce his heart.

Please, Virgin Mary, you, too, shelter him. Shield his body, cover his head, cover the eyes of the Communists and the Koreans and the Chinese so that they cannot see him, so they won't kill him. I still keep his toys from when he was a child, his little cars, little trucks, even a kite that I found the other day in the closet. Also his cards and the funnies that he has learned to read. I have put everything away until his return.

Protect him, Jesus, that they may not kill him. I have made a promise to the Virgen de San Juan to pay her homage at her shrine and to the Virgen de Guadalupe, too. He also wears a little medallion of the Virgen de San Juan del Valle and he, too, has made a promise to her; he wants to live. Take care of him, cover his heart with your hand, that no bullet may enter it. He's very noble. He was very afraid to go, he told me so. The day they took him, when he said his farewell he embraced me and he cried for a while. I could feel his heart beating and I remembered when he was little and I would nurse him and the happiness that I felt and he felt.

Take care of him for me, please, I beseech you. I promise you my life for his. Bring him back from Korea safe and sound. Cover his heart with your hands. Jesus Christ, Holy God, Virgen de Guadalupe, bring him back alive, bring me back his heart. Why have they taken him? He has done no harm. He knows nothing. He is very humble. He doesn't want to take away anybody's life. Bring him back alive, I don't want him to die.

Here is my heart for his. Here is my heart. Here, in my chest, palpitating. Tear it out if blood is what you want, but tear it out of *me*. I sacrifice my heart for his. Here it is. Here is my heart! Through it runs his very own blood . . .

Bring him back alive and I will give you my very own heart.

"Comadre, do you all plan to go to Utah?"

"No, compadre. I'll tell you, we don't trust the man that's contracting people to go work in—how do you say it?"

"Utah. Why, comadre?"

"Because we don't think there's such a state. You tell me, when've you ever heard of that place?"

"Well, there's so many states. And this is the first time that they've contracted for work in those parts."

"Yeah, but tell me, where is it?"

"Well, we've never been there but I hear it's somewhere close to Japan."

It's That It Hurts

It hurts a lot. That's why I hit him. And now what do I do? Maybe they didn't expel me from school. Maybe it ain't so, after all. Maybe it's not. *Sure it is!* It is so, they did expel me. And now what do I do?

I think it all started when I got so embarrassed and angry at the same time. I dread getting home. What am I going to tell Mother? And then when Dad gets home from the fields? They'll whip me for sure. But it's embarrassing and angering. It's always the same in these schools in the north. Everybody just stares at you up and down. And then they make fun of you and the teacher with her popsicle stick, poking your head for lice. It's embarrassing. And then when they turn up their noses. It makes you angry. I think it's better staying out here on the ranch, here in the quiet of this knoll, with its chicken coops, or out in the fields where you at least feel more free, more at ease.

"Come on, son, we're almost there."

"You gonna take me to the principal?"

"Of course not. Don't tell me you don't know how to speak English yet. Look, that's the entrance over there. Just ask if you don't know where to go. Don't be shy, ask someone. Don't be afraid."

"Why can't you go in with me?"

"Don't tell me you're scared. Look, that's probably the entrance there. Here comes someone. Now, you behave, you hear me?"

"But why don't you help me?"

"No. You'll do just fine, don't be afraid."

It's always the same. They take you to the nurse and the first thing she does is check you for lice. And, too, those ladies are to blame. On Sundays they sit out in front of the chicken coops picking lice from each other's heads. And the gringos, passing by in their cars, looking and pointing at them. Dad is right when he says that they look like monkeys in the zoo. But it's not all that bad.

"Mother, you won't believe it. They took me out of the room. I had just walked in, and they put me in with a nurse all dressed in white. And they made me take off my clothes and they even examined my behind. But where they took the longest was on my head. I had washed it, right? Well, the nurse brought out a jar of, like vaseline, it smelled like worm-killer, do I still smell? And she smeared it all over my head. It itched. And then she started parting my hair with a pencil. After a while they let me go but I was so ashamed because I had to take off my pants, even my underwear, in front of the nurse."

But now what do I tell them? That they threw me out of school? But it wasn't all my fault. I didn't like that gringo, right off. This one didn't laugh at me. He'd just stare and when they put me in the corner apart from everyone he kept turning to look at me, and then he'd make a gesture with his finger. I was mad but mostly I felt embarrassed because I was sitting away from everyone where they could see me better. Then when it was my turn to read, I couldn't. I could hear myself. And I could hear that no words were coming out . . . This cemetery isn't scary at all. That's what I like best about the walk to school and back. The greenness! And everything so even. The roads all paved. It even looks like where they play golf. Today I won't have time to run up the hills and slide down tumbling. Nor to lie down on the grass and try to hear all the sounds. Last time I counted to 26 . . . If I hurry maybe I can go to the dump with Doña Cuquita. She heads out about this time when the sun's not so hot.

"Careful, children. Just be careful and don't step where there's fire burning underneath. Wherever you see smoke coming out, there's coals underneath. I know what I'm telling you, I once got a bad burn and I still have the scar . . . Look, each of you get a long stick and just turn the trash over briskly. If the dump man comes to see what we're doing, tell him we came to throw away some stuff. He's a kind man, but he likes to keep those little books with nasty pictures that people sometimes throw away . . . watch out for the train as you cross that bridge. It ran over a man last year . . . caught him right in the middle of the bridge and he wasn't able to make it to the other side . . . Did they give you permission to come with me? . . . Don't eat anything until after you've washed it."

But if I go with her without permission they'll whip me even more. What am I going to tell them? Maybe they didn't expel me. *Sure, they did!* Maybe not. *Yeah, they did!* What am I going to tell them? But it wasn't all my fault. I couldn't wait anymore. While I was standing there in the restroom he's the one that started picking on me.

"Hey, Mex . . . I don't like Mexicans because they steal. You hear me?"
"Yes."
"I don't like Mexicans. You hear, Mex?"
"Yes."

"I don't like Mexicans because they steal. You hear me?"

"Yes."

I remember the first fight I had at school, I got real scared because everything happened so slow. There wasn't any reason, it's just that some of the older boys who already had mustaches and who were still in the second grade started pushing us against each other. And they kept it up until we started fighting, I think, 'cause we were plain scared. It was about a block from school, I remember, when they started pushing me towards Ramiro. Then we began to scuffle and hit at each other. Some ladies came out and broke us up. Since then I got to feeling bigger. But all it was, up until I fought, was plain fear.

This time it was different. He didn't warn me. I just felt a real hard blow on my ear and I heard something like when you put a conch to your ear at the beach. I don't remember anymore how or when I hit him but I know I did because someone told the principal that we were fighting in the restroom. Maybe they didn't throw me out? *Sure they did!* And then, I wonder who called the principal? And the janitor all scared and with his broom up in the air, ready to swat me if I tried to leave.

"The Mexican kid got into a fight and beat up a couple of our boys . . . No, not bad . . . but what do I do?"

". . ."

"No, I guess not, they could care less if I expel him . . . They need him in the fields."

". . ."

"Well, I just hope our boys don't make too much out about it to their parents. I guess I'll just throw him out."

". . ."

"Yeah, I guess you're right."

". . ."

"I know you warned me, I know, I know . . . but . . . yeah, ok."

But how could I even think of leaving knowing that everyone at home wanted me to go to school. Anyways, the janitor stood with his broom up in the air, ready for anything . . . And then they just told me to leave.

I'm halfway home. This cemetery is real pretty. It doesn't look anything like the one in Texas. That one *is* scary, I don't like it at all. What scares me the most is when we're leaving after a burial and I look up and I read the letters on the arch over the gate that say, *Don't forget me.* It's like I can hear all the dead people buried there saying these words and then the sound of these words stays in my mind and sometimes even if I don't look up when I pass through the gate, I still see them. But not this one, this one is real pretty. Just lots of soft grass and trees, I guess that's why here when people bury somebody they don't even cry. I like playing here. If only they would let us fish in the little creek that runs through here, there's lots of fish. But no, you even need a license to fish and then they don't even sell us one 'cause we're from out of state.

I won't be able to go to school anymore. What am I going to tell them? They've told me over and over that our teachers are like our second parents . . . and now? And when we get back to Texas everyone will find out too. Mother and Dad will be angry; I might get more than just a whipping. And then my Uncle will find out and Grandpa. Maybe they might even send me to a reform school like the ones I've heard them talk about. There they turn you into a good person if you're bad. They're real hard on you. They leave you soft as a glove. But maybe they didn't expel me, *sure they did*, maybe not, *sure they did*. I could make like I'm going to school and stay here in the cemetery. That would be better. But then what? I could tell them that I lost my report card. And then what if I stay in the same grade? What hurt me the most is that now I won't be able to be a telephone operator like Dad wants me to. You need to finish school for that.

"Vieja, call m'ijo out here . . . look, compadre, ask your godson what he wants to be when he grows up and finishes school."
"What will you be, godson?"
"I don't know."
"Tell him! Don't be embarrassed. He's your godfather."
"What will you be, son?"
"A telephone operator."
"Is that so?"
"Yes, compadre, he's very determined, you know that? Every time we ask him he says he wants to be an operator. I think they pay well. I told the boss the other day and he laughed. I don't think he believes that my son can do it, but that's 'cause he doesn't know him. He's smarter than anything. I just pray God helps him finish school so he can become an operator."

That movie was good. The operator was the most important one. Ever since then I suppose that's why Dad has wanted me to study for that after I finish school. But . . . maybe they didn't throw me out. What if it's not true? Maybe not. *Sure, it is.* What do I tell them? What do I do? Now they won't be able to ask me what I'm going to be when I grow up. Maybe not. *No, yeah.* What do I do? It's that it hurts and it's embarrassing at the same time. I better just stay here.

No, but then Mother will get scared like she does when there's lightning and thunder. I've gotta tell them. And when my padrino comes to visit us I'll just hide. No need for him to find out. Nor for me to read to him like Dad has me do every time he comes to visit us. What I'll do when he comes is hide behind the chest or under the bed. That way Dad and Mother won't feel embarrassed. And what if I really wasn't expelled? Maybe I wasn't? *No, yeah.*

"Why do y'all go to school so much?"

"My Dad says it's to prepare us. He says that if someday there's an opportunity, maybe they'll give it to us."

"Sure! If I were you I wouldn't worry about that. The poor can't get poorer. We can't get worst off than we already are. That's why I don't worry. The ones who have to be on their toes are the ones who are higher up. They've got something to lose. They can end up where we're at. But for us what does it matter?"

Hand in His Pocket

〰️

Remember Don Laíto and Doña Bone? That's what everyone called them but their names were Don Hilario and Doña Bonifacia. Don't you remember? Well, I had to live with them for three weeks until school ended. At first I liked it but then later on I didn't.

Everything that people used to say about them behind their backs was true. About how they baked the bread, the pastries, how they would sometimes steal and that they were bootleggers. I saw it all. Anyways, they were good people but by the time school was about to end I was afraid of being with them in that Model-T that they had and even of sleeping in their house. And towards the end I didn't even feel like eating. That's why I'd go to the little neighborhood store to buy me some candy. And that's how I got along until my Dad, my Mother and my brothers and sisters came to get me.

I remember they were very nice to me on the first day. Don Laíto laughed a lot and you could see his gold teeth and the rotten ones, too. And every little while Doña Bone, fat as could be, would grab me and squeeze me against her and I could feel her, real fat. They fed me dinner—I say *fed* me because *they* didn't eat. Now that I'm remembering, you know, I never saw them eat. The meat that she fried for me was green and it smelled really bad when she was cooking it. But after a while it didn't smell as much. But I don't know whether this was because I got used to the smell or because Don Laíto opened the window. Just parts of it tasted bad. I ate it all because I didn't want to hurt their feelings. Everybody liked Don Laíto and Doña Bone. Even the Anglos were fond of them. They gave them canned foods, clothes, toys. And when Don

Laíto and Doña Bone weren't able to sell these to us, they'd give them to us. They would also pay us visits out in the fields to sell us Mexican sweet bread, thread and needles, canned food and nopalitos, and also shoes, coats and other things that sometimes were good, sometimes pretty bad.

"Won't you buy these shoes . . . oh, come on . . . I know they're used, but they're the expensive kind . . . look how they're not worn out yet . . . these . . . I guarantee you, they last until they wear out . . ."

I didn't want to seem ungrateful, so I ate it all. It made me sick. I had to spend a long time in the restroom. The worst of it was when I went to bed. They put me in a room with no light and that smelled musty and was crowded with things: boxes, bottles, almanacs, bundles of clothing. There was only one entrance. You couldn't even see the windows with so many things all piled up. The first night I hardly slept because I was sure that spiders would be crawling down from the hole in the ceiling. Everything smelled so awful. By the time it grew dark I couldn't see anything, but it must have been around midnight when I woke up. I think I had fallen asleep, but I'm not too sure. The only thing I could see was that real dark hole in the ceiling. It seemed I could see faces but it was just my imagination. In any case, fear got the best of me. And I wasn't able to sleep anymore. Only at dawn when I could see the rest of the things in the room. Sometimes I would imagine Don Laíto and Doña Bone seated around me and there were times when I would even reach my hand out to touch them, but there was nothing. I think that from that very first day I wanted them to come get me. Something in my heart told me that something would happen. It's not that they weren't good people, they were, but like they say, they had their bad side.

At school, classes were going well. Sometimes when I came back from school in the afternoon not a sound could be heard in the small house and it seemed like no one was around. But always, when I was feeling most at peace, Doña Bone would scare me. She'd grab me from behind and laugh, and me, I'd jump, I was so scared. And she would just laugh and laugh. The first few times I'd end up laughing too, but later I got tired of it. Then later on they told me bit by bit what they would do when they went downtown. They stole lots of things: food, liquor, clothes, cigarettes, even meat. When they weren't able to sell it to the neighbors, they gave it away. They would get rid of almost everything. Another thing, after a few days they invited me to see how they made sweet bread. Don Laíto would take off his shirt. He looked very hairy. He would start sweating as he kneaded the dough. But it was when he would stick his hands under his arms and then keep on kneading the dough that made me the sickest. It was true what people said. He would look at me to see if I was getting nauseous and he would tell me that this was what all the bakers did. One thing for sure, I never again ate any of the sweet bread that he baked, even though they sometimes had a bunch of it on the table.

I remember one day after school they put me to work in the yard. Not that it was so hard, but since that moment they had me working all the time. They wanted me to work at all hours. It's that my Dad had paid them for my board! One time they even wanted me to try to steal a five-pound sack of flour. Can you imagine? I was scared, and besides, it wasn't right. Don Laíto would just laugh and tell me that I didn't have any balls. Anyway, the days went on this way until, sometimes, I even felt like leaving, but how could I? My Dad had left me there and he had spent his money. The food got worse, and it got to be all work all the time.

And then . . . I'll tell you something . . . but please don't tell anyone. I noticed that this wetback started coming to the house while Don Laíto was away. I don't know how he knew when he wasn't there. Anyway, if I happened to be inside the house, Doña Bone would throw me out, and if I wasn't inside she would latch the doors and I knew I wasn't supposed to enter. One time Doña Bone tried to explain the whole thing to me but, to be very honest, I felt embarrassed and I hardly heard anything she told me. I did know that he left her money. Whoever he was, he was old and every time he came he smelled of shaving lotion and the smell would linger for a good while after he left. One night I overheard a conversation between the old couple.

"This guy has money and, besides that, he doesn't have any relatives. Look, viejo, it would be so easy. Not even anyone to worry about him . . . I don't think so, do you? . . . That boss could care less, he darn sure knows that he's a wetback and if something happens to him, you think he'll be concerned about him? Nobody knows that he comes here . . . you just leave it up to me . . . Oh, that'll be so easy . . ."

The next day, after school, they marked a square on the ground in the yard under some trees, and they told me that they wanted to build a cellar and that they wanted me to start digging there, little by little. They were going to use it to store the jars of preserves that Doña Bone made. It took me three days to dig somewhat deep and then they told me to stop digging, that they weren't going to build it after all. And then came the good part.

I remember well that the wetback arrived, his hair combed real good and fragrant, like always. At dusk Doña Bone called me to come eat. There was Don Laíto, already, but I didn't know how he had entered. After dinner they told me to go to bed right away.

I got the scare of my life when I stretched out on the bed and I touched what felt like a snake but what was in reality the wetback's arm. I thought he must be drunk because he didn't wake up. I jumped back and got out of the room. The old couple burst into laughter. Then I noticed that part of my shirt was full of blood. I didn't know what to think. I just remember Don Laíto's gold teeth and his rotten ones.

When it got real dark they made me help them drag him out and throw him into the hole that I myself had dug. As for me, I didn't really want to but then they told me that they would tell the police that I had killed him. I thought of how my Dad had paid them for my room and board and how even the Anglos liked them so much. All that my parents wanted was for me to finish school so I could find me some job that wasn't so hard. I was real scared but I went ahead and threw him in the hole. Then the three of us threw dirt over him. I never saw his face. All I wanted was for school to end so they would come for me. The two weeks left went by very slowly. I thought that I'd get over my fright or that I'd be able to forget about it, but no. Don Laíto was even wearing the wetback's wristwatch. In the yard you could see the mound of dirt.

When my Dad and my Mother finally came for me they told me that I was very thin and that I looked like I was sick from fright. I told them no, that it was because I played so much at school and after school. Before we left, Don Laíto and Doña Bone squeezed me and told me in loud voices, so that Dad could hear, not to say anything or they would tell the police. Then they started laughing and I noticed that Dad had taken it as a joke. On the way to the farm they talked about how kind Don Laíto and Doña Bone were and how everyone liked them so much. I just kept looking out the car window and telling them yes. After about two months or so, just about when it seemed that I was forgetting all about it, they came to visit us at the farm. They had a present for me. A ring. They made me put it on and I remembered that it was the one the wetback had on that day. As soon as they left I tried to throw it away but I don't know why I couldn't. I thought that someone might find it. And the worst was that for a long time, as soon as I would see a stranger, I'd slip my hand into my pocket. That habit stayed with me for a long time.

It was an hour before the afternoon movie started. He needed a haircut, so he went into the barber shop across the street from the theater. At first he didn't quite understand, so he sat down and waited. But then the barber told him again that he couldn't cut his hair. He thought the barber didn't have time, so he remained seated waiting for the other barber. When he was finished with the client, he got up and walked to the barber's chair. But this barber told him the same thing. That he couldn't cut his hair. Furthermore, he told him that it would be better if he left. He crossed the street and stood there waiting for the theater to open, but then the barber came out and told him to leave. Then it all became clear to him and he went home to get his father.

A Silvery Night

〜

It was a silvery night when he called the devil.
Everything was almost clear and it even smelled like
day. The whole day he thought about what could
happen to him, but the more he thought about it the
more curious he became and the less fearful. So that
by the time everybody went to bed and turned off the
lights, he had already decided to go out right at
midnight. He would have to slide across the floor to
the door without anyone hearing or seeing him.

"Dad. Why don't you leave the door open.
There aren't any mosquitos, anyway."
"Yes, but what if some animal gets in. You
remember that badger that got into the Flores'
home."
"But that was two years ago. Come on, leave
it open. It's real hot. Nothing's gonna get in. All
that's left around here are crows, and those don't
get into people's houses. Come on. See how all
the other people leave their doors open."
"Yes, but at least they've got screens."
"Not all of them. Please. See how pretty the
moon looks. Everything is so peaceful."
"All right . . . No, Vieja, no animal is going
to crawl in. You and your fears."

The devil had fascinated him as far back as he could
remember. Even when they had taken him to the
shepherds plays at his Aunt Pana's, he was already
curious about how it might look. He thought about
Don Rayos, with his black metal mask, with his red
horns and black cape. Then he remembered how he
found the costume and the mask under Don Rayos'
house. One of his marbles had rolled under the house

and when he reached for it he found everything all full of dust. He pulled everything out, dusted it off and then he put on the mask.

"I tell you, compadre, you don't fool around with the devil. There are many who have summoned him and have regretted it afterwards. Most of them go insane. Sometimes they get together in groups to summon him, so they won't be afraid. But he doesn't appear before them until later, when each of them is alone, and he appears in different shapes. No, nobody should fool with the devil. If you do, as they say, you give up your soul. Some die of fright, others don't. They just start looking real somber and then they don't even talk anymore. It's like their spirits have left their bodies."

From where he was lying on the floor he could see the clock on the table. He sensed each of his brothers and sisters falling asleep, one by one, and then his parents. He thought he could even make out the sound of snores coming from the other chicken shacks. Eleven to eleven-fifty went by the slowest. Occasionally, he felt somewhat fearful, but then he would look outside where everything was so still and serene under the silvery light of the moon and his fears quickly passed.

"If I leave here at eleven-fifty I'll have enough time to get to the center of the knoll. Good thing there's no snakes here, otherwise it'd be dangerous walking through the weeds that grow so tall at the center of the knoll. I'll call him right at twelve. I better take the clock so I'll know when it's exactly twelve. Otherwise, he might not come. It has to be right at midnight, exactly midnight."

Very slowly, without making a sound, he left, picking up the clock from the table. He put it in his pants' pocket and he noticed that it ticked louder inside the pocket than outside. Even once he was past the chicken coops he walked very slowly, stepping carefully and stopping every now and then. He felt someone was watching him. He proceeded cautiously until he had passed the outhouse. From there the chicken coops were barely visible and he began talking to himself but very softly.

"And how do I call him? Maybe he'll appear. No, I don't think so. In any case, if he does appear he can't do anything to me. I haven't died yet. So he can't do anything to me. I'd just like to know whether there is or isn't . . . If there isn't a devil, maybe there also isn't . . . No, I better not say it. I might get punished. But if there's no devil maybe there's no punishment. No, there has to be punishment. Well, how do I call him? Just, devil? Or, imp? Or, demon? Lucifer? Satan? . . . Whatever comes first."

He got to the center of the knoll and summoned him. At first no words came out, from pure fright, but then his name slipped out in a loud voice and nothing happened. He kept calling him by different names. And nothing. No one came out. Everything looked the same. Everything was the same. All peaceful. Then he thought it would be better to curse the devil instead. So he did. He swore at him using all the cuss words that he knew and in different tones of voice. He even cursed the devil's mother. But nothing. Nothing nor no one appeared, nor did anything change. Disillusioned and feeling at moments a little brave, he headed back for the house. The sound of the wind rustling the leaves of the trees seemed to accompany his every step. There was no devil.

"But if there's no devil neither is there . . . No, I better not say it. I might get punished. But there's no devil. Maybe he'll appear before me later. No, he would've appeared already. What better time than at night and me, alone? No, there's no devil. There isn't."

Two or three different times he sensed someone calling him but he didn't want to turn around. He didn't get scared because he felt sure that it wasn't anyone nor anything. After he laid down, very careful not to make a sound, certain that there was no devil, he began to feel chills and his stomach became upset. Before falling asleep he thought for a good while. *There is no devil, there is nothing.* The only thing that had been present in the woods was his own voice. No wonder, he thought, people said you shouldn't fool around with the devil. Now he understood everything. Those who summoned the devil went crazy, not because the devil appeared, but just the opposite, because he didn't appear. He fell asleep gazing at the moon as it jumped through the clouds and the trees, as if it were extremely content about something.

One afternoon a minister from one of the protestant churches in the town came to the farm and informed them that some man would be coming to teach them manual skills so that they would no longer have to work just in the fields. Practically all of the men got excited. He was going to teach them carpentry. A man came about two weeks later in a station wagon hauling a trailer. He brought with him the minister's wife to assist him as interpreter. But they never taught them anything. They would spend the entire day inside the trailer. A week later they left without a word. They later learned that the man had run off with the minister's wife.

. . . *And the Earth Did Not Devour Him*

〜

The first time he felt hate and anger was when he saw his mother crying for his uncle and his aunt. They both had caught tuberculosis and had been sent to different sanitariums. So, between the brothers and sisters, they had split up the children among themselves and had taken care of them as best they could. Then the aunt died, and soon thereafter they brought the uncle back from the sanitarium, but he was already spitting blood. That was when he saw his mother crying every little while. He became angry because he was unable to do anything against anyone. Today he felt the same. Only today it was for his father.

"You all should've come home right away, m'ijo. Couldn't you see that your Daddy was sick? You should have known that he'd suffered a sunstroke. Why didn't you come home?"

"I don't know. Us being so soaked with sweat, we didn't feel so hot, but I guess that when you're sunstruck it's different. But I did tell him to sit down under the tree that's at the edge of the rows, but he didn't want to. And that was when he started throwing up. Then we saw he couldn't hoe anymore and we dragged him and put him under a tree. He didn't put up a fuss at that point. He just let us take him. He didn't even say a word."

"Poor viejo, my poor viejo. Last night he hardly slept. Didn't you hear him outside the house? He squirmed in bed all night with cramps. God willing, he'll get well. I've been giving him cool lemonade all day, but his eyes still look glassy. If I'd gone to the fields yesterday,

I tell you, he wouldn't have gotten sick. My poor viejo, he's going to have cramps all over his body for three days and three nights at the least. Now, you all take care of yourselves. Don't overwork yourselves so much. Don't pay any mind to that boss if he tries to rush you. Just don't do it. He thinks it's so easy since he's not the one who's out there stooped."

He became even angrier when he heard his father moan outside the chicken coop. He wouldn't stay inside because he said it made him feel very anxious. Outside where he could feel the fresh air was where he got some relief. And also when the cramps came he could roll over on the grass. Then he thought about whether his father might die from the sunstroke. At times he heard his father start to pray and ask for God's help. At first he had faith that he would get well soon but by the next day he felt the anger growing inside of him. And all the more when he heard his mother and his father clamoring for God's mercy. That night, well past midnight, he had been awakened by his father's groans. His mother got up and removed the scapularies from around his neck and washed them. Then she lit some candles. But nothing happened. It was like his aunt and uncle all over again.

"What's to be gained from doing all that, Mother? Don't tell me you think it helped my aunt and uncle any. How come we're like this, like we're buried alive? Either the germs eat us alive or the sun burns us up. Always some kind of sickness. And every day we work and work. For what? Poor Dad, always working so hard. I think he was born working. Like he says, barely five years old and already helping his father plant corn. All the time feeding the earth and the sun, only to one day, just like that, get struck down by the sun. And there you are, helpless. And them, begging for God's help . . . why, God doesn't care about us . . . I don't think there even is . . . No, better not say it, what if Dad gets worse. Poor Dad, I guess that at least gives him some hope."

His mother noticed how furious he was, and that morning she told him to calm down, that everything was in God's hands and that with God's help his father was going to get well.

"Oh, Mother, do you really believe that? I am certain that God has no concern for us. Now you tell me, is Dad evil or mean-hearted? You tell me if he has ever done any harm to anyone."

"Of course not."

"So there you have it. You see? And my aunt and uncle? You explain. And the poor kids, now orphans, never having known their parents. Why did God have to take them away? I tell you, God could care less about the poor. Tell me, why must we live here like this? What have we done to deserve this? You're so good and yet you have to suffer so much."

"Oh, please, m'ijo, don't talk that way. Don't speak against the will of God. Don't talk that way, please, m'ijo. You scare me. It's as if already the blood of Satan runs through your veins."

"Well, maybe. That way at least, I could get rid of this anger. I'm so tired of thinking about it. Why? Why you? Why Dad? Why my uncle? Why my aunt? Why their kids? Tell me, Mother, why? Why us, burrowed in the dirt like animals with no hope for anything? You know the only hope we have is coming out here every year. And like you yourself say, only death brings rest. I think that's the way my aunt and uncle felt and that's how Dad must feel too."

"That's how it is, m'ijo. Only death brings us rest."

"But why us?"

"Well, they say that . . ."

"Don't say it. I know what you're going to tell me—that the poor go to heaven."

That day started out cloudy and he could feel the morning coolness brushing his eyelashes as he and his brothers and sisters began the day's labor. Their mother had to stay home to care for her husband. Thus, he felt responsible for hurrying on his brothers and sisters. During the morning, at least for the first few hours, they endured the heat but by ten-thirty the sun had suddenly cleared the skies and pressed down against the world. They began working more slowly because of the weakness, dizziness and suffocation they felt when they worked too fast. Then they had to wipe the sweat from their eyes every little while because their vision would get blurred.

"If you start blacking out, stop working, you hear me? Or go a little slower. When we reach the edge we'll rest a bit to get our strength back. It's gonna be hot today. If only it'd stay just a bit cloudy like this morning, then nobody would complain. But no, once the sun bears down like this not even one little cloud dares to appear out of fear. And the worst of it is we'll finish up here by two and then we have to go over to that other field that's nothing but hills. It's okay at the top of the hill but down in the lower part of the slopes it gets to be real suffocating. There's no breeze there. Hardly any air goes through. Remember?"

"Yeah."

"That's where the hottest part of the day will catch us. Just drink plenty of water every little while. It don't matter if the boss gets mad. Just don't get sick. And if you can't go on, tell me right away, all right? We'll go home. Y'all saw what happened to Dad when he pushed himself too hard. The sun has no mercy, it can eat you alive."

Just as they had figured, they had moved on to the other field by early afternoon. By three o'clock they were all soaked with sweat. Not one part of their clothing was dry. Every little while they would stop. At times they could barely breathe, then they would black out and they would become fearful of getting sunstruck, but they kept on working.

"How do y'all feel?"

"Man, it's so hot! But we've got to keep on. 'Til six, at least. Except this water don't help our thirst any. Sure wish I had a bottle of cool water, real cool, fresh from the well, or a coke ice-cold."

"Are you crazy? That'd sure make you sunsick right now. Just don't work so fast. Let's see if we can make it until six. What do you think?"

At four o'clock the youngest became ill. He was only nine years old, but since he was paid the same as a grownup he tried to keep up with the rest. He began vomiting. He sat down, then he laid down. Terrified, the other children ran to where he lay and looked at him. It appeared that he had fainted and when they opened his eyelids they saw his eyes were rolled back. The next youngest child started crying but right away he told him to stop and help him carry his brother home. It seemed he was having cramps all over his little body. He lifted him and carried him by himself and, again, he began asking himself *why?*

"Why Dad and then my little brother? He's only nine years old. Why? He has to work like a mule buried in the earth. Dad, Mom, and my little brother here, what are they guilty of?"

Each step that he took towards the house resounded with the question, *why?* About halfway to the house he began to get furious. Then he started crying out of rage. His little brothers and sisters did not know what to do, and they, too, started crying, but out of fear. Then he started cursing. And without even realizing it, he said what he had been wanting to say for a long time. He cursed God. Upon doing this he felt that fear instilled in him by the years and by his parents. For a second he saw the earth opening up to devour him. Then he felt his footsteps against the earth, compact, more solid than ever. Then his anger swelled up again and he vented it by cursing God. He looked at his brother, he no longer looked sick. He didn't know whether his brothers and sisters had understood the graveness of his curse.

That night he did not fall asleep until very late. He felt at peace as never before. He felt as though he had become detached from everything. He no longer worried about his father nor his brother. All that he awaited was the new day, the freshness of the morning. By daybreak his father was doing better. He was on his way to recovery. And his little brother, too; the cramps had almost completely subsided. Frequently he felt a sense of surprise upon recalling what he had done the previous afternoon. He thought of telling his mother, but he decided to keep it secret. All he told her was that the earth did not devour anyone, nor did the sun.

He left for work and encountered a very cool morning. There were clouds in the sky and for the first time he felt capable of doing and undoing anything that he pleased. He looked down at the earth and kicked it hard and said:

"Not yet, you can't swallow me up yet. Someday, yes. But I'll never know it."

A stroke left the grandfather paralyzed from the neck down. One day one of his grandsons came by to visit with him. The grandfather asked him how old he was and what he most desired in life. The grandson replied that what he most wanted was for the next ten years to pass by immediately so that he would know what had happened in his life. The grandfather told him he was very stupid and cut off the conversation. The grandson did not understand why he had called him stupid until he turned thirty.

First Communion

The priest always held First Communion during mid-spring. I'll always remember that day in my life. I remember what I was wearing and I remember my godfather and the pastries and chocolate that we had after mass, but I also remember what I saw at the cleaners that was next to the church. I think it all happened because I left so early for church. It's that I hadn't been able to sleep the night before, trying to remember all of my sins, and worse yet, trying to arrive at an exact number. Furthermore, since Mother had placed a picture of hell at the head of the bed and since the walls of the room were papered with images of the devil and since I wanted salvation from all evil, that was all I could think of.

"Remember, children, very quiet, very, very quiet. You have learned your prayers well, and now you know which are the mortal sins and which are the venial sins, now you know what sacrilege is, now you know that you are God's children, but you can also be children of the devil. When you go to confession you must tell all of your sins, you must try to remember all of the sins you have committed. Because if you forget one and receive Holy Communion then that would be a sacrilege and if you commit sacrilege you will go to hell. God knows all. You cannot lie to God. You can lie to me and to the priest, but God knows everything; so if your soul is not pure of sin, then you should not receive Holy Communion. That would be a sacrilege. So everyone confess all of your sins. Recall all of your sins. Wouldn't you be ashamed if you received Holy Communion and then later remembered a sin that you had forgotten to confess? Now, let's see, let us practice confessing our sins. Who would like to start off? Let us begin with the sins that we commit with our hands when we touch our bodies. Who would like to start?"

The nun liked for us to talk about the sins of the flesh. The real truth was that we practiced a lot telling our sins, but the real truth was that I didn't understand a lot of things. What did scare me was the idea of going to hell because some months earlier I had fallen against a small basin filled with hot coals which we used as a heater in the little room where we slept. I had burned my calf. I could well imagine how it might be to burn in hell forever. That was all that I understood. So I spent that night, the eve of my First Communion, going over all the sins I had committed. But what was real hard was coming up with the exact number like the nun wanted us to. It must have been dawn by the time I finally satisfied my conscience. I had committed one hundred and fifty sins, but I was going to admit to two hundred.

"If I say one hundred and fifty and I've forgotten some, that would be bad. I'll just say two-hundred and that way even if I forget lots of them I won't commit any kind of sacrilege. Yes, I have committed two hundred sins . . . Father, I have come to confess my sins . . . How many? . . . Two hundred . . . of all kinds . . . The Commandments? Against all of the Ten Commandments . . . This way there will be no sacrilege. It's better this way. By confessing more sins you'll be purer."

I remember I got up much earlier that morning than Mother had expected. My godfather would be waiting for me at the church and I didn't want to be even one second late.

"Hurry, Mother, get my pants ready, I thought you already ironed them last night."

"It's just that I couldn't see anymore last night. My eyesight is failing me now and that's why I had to leave them for this morning. But tell me, what's your hurry now? It's still very early. Confession isn't until eight o'clock and it's only six. Your padrino won't be there until eight."

"I know, but I couldn't sleep. Hurry, Mother, I want to leave now."

"And what are you going to do there so early?"

"Well, I want to leave because I'm afraid I'll forget the sins I have to confess to the priest. I can think better at the church."

"All right, I'll be through in just a minute. Believe me, as long as I can see I'm able to do a lot."

I headed for church repeating my sins and reciting the Holy Sacraments. The morning was already bright and clear but there weren't many people out in the street yet. The morning was cool. When I got to the church I found that it was closed. I think the priest might have overslept or was very busy. That was why I walked around the church and passed by the cleaners that was next to the church. The sound of loud laughter and moans surprised me because I didn't expect anybody to be in there. I thought it might be a dog but then it sounded like people again and that's why I peeked in through the little window in the door. They didn't see me but I saw them. They were naked and embracing each other, lying on some shirts and dresses on the floor. I don't know why but I couldn't move away from the window. Then they saw me and tried to cover themselves, and they yelled at me to get out of there. The woman's hair looked all messed up and she looked like she was sick. And me, to tell the truth, I got scared and ran to the church but I couldn't get my mind off of what I had seen. I realized then that maybe those were the sins that we committed with our hands. But I couldn't forget the sight of that woman and that man lying on the floor. When my friends started arriving I was going to tell them but then I thought it would be better to tell them after communion. More and more I was feeling like I was the one who had committed a sin of the flesh.

"There's nothing I can do now. But I can't tell the others 'cause they'll sin like me. I better not go to communion. Better that I don't go to confession. I can't, now that I know, I can't. But what will Mom and Dad say if I don't go to communion? And my padrino, I can't leave him there waiting. I have to confess what I saw. I feel like going back. Maybe they're still there on the floor. No choice, I'm gonna have to lie. What if I forget it between now and confession? Maybe I didn't see anything? And if I hadn't seen anything?"

I remember that when I went in to confess and the priest asked for my sins, all I told him was two hundred and of all kinds. I did not confess the sin of the flesh. On returning to the house with my godfather, everything seemed changed, like I was and yet wasn't in the same place. Everything seemed smaller and less important. When I saw my Dad and my Mother, I imagined them on the floor. I started seeing all of the grownups naked and their faces even looked distorted, and I could even hear them laughing and moaning, even though they weren't even laughing. Then I started imagining the priest and the nun on the floor. I couldn't hardly eat any of the sweet bread or drink the chocolate. As soon as I finished, I recall running out of the house. It felt like I couldn't breathe.

"So, what's the matter with him? Such manners!"

"Ah, compadre, let him be. You don't have to be concerned on my account. I have my own. These young ones, all they can think about is playing. Let him have a good time, it's the day of his First Communion."

"Sure, compadre, I'm not saying they shouldn't play. But they have to learn to be more courteous. They have to show more respect toward adults, their elders, and all the more for their padrino."

"No, well, that's true."

I remember I headed toward the thicket. I picked up some rocks and threw them at the cactus. Then I broke some bottles. I climbed a tree and stayed there for a long time until I got tired of thinking. I kept remembering the scene at the cleaners, and there, alone, I even liked recalling it. I even forgot that I had lied to the priest. And then I felt the same as I once had when I had heard a missionary speak about the grace of God. I felt like knowing more about everything. And then it occurred to me that maybe everything was the same.

The teacher was surprised when, hearing that they needed a button on the poster to represent the button industry, the child tore one off his shirt and offered it to her. She was surprised because she knew that this was probably the only shirt the child had. She didn't know whether he did this to be helpful, to feel like he belonged or out of love for her. She did feel the intensity of the child's desire and this was what surprised her most of all.

The Little Burnt Victims

~≫

There were five in the García family. Don Efraín,
Doña Chona and their three children: Raulito, Juan
and María—seven, six and five years old, respectively.
On Sunday evening they arrived from the theater
excited over the movie about boxing that they had
seen. Don Efraín was the most excited. When they
arrived, he brought out the boxing gloves he had
bought for the children and then he made them put
them on. He even stripped them down to their shorts
and rubbed a bit of alcohol on their little chests, just
like they had seen done in the movie. Doña Chona
didn't like for them to box because someone would
always end up getting mad and then the wailing
would start and last for a long time.

> "That's enough, viejo. Why do you make
> them fight? Remember how Juan's nose always
> starts to bleed and you know how hard it is to
> make the bleeding stop. Come on, viejo, let them
> go to bed."
> "Man, vieja!"
> "I'm not a man."
> "Oh, let them fight. Maybe they'll at least
> learn how to defend themselves."
> "But can't you see that we barely have
> enough room to stand up in this chicken shack
> and there you are running around like we had so
> much space."
> "And what do you think they do when we go
> to work? I wish they were older so we could take
> them with us to the fields. They could work or at
> least sit quietly in the car."
> "Yeah, but do you really think so? The older
> they get, the more restless they become. I don't

like it at all leaving them here by themselves."

"Maybe one of them will turn out good with the glove, and then we'll be set vieja. Just think how much money champions win. Thousands and thousands. I'm gonna see if I can order them a punching bag through the catalog next week, as soon as we get paid."

"Well, true. You never know, right?"

"Right. That's what I'm telling you."

The three children were left to themselves in the house when they went to work because the owner didn't like children in the fields doing mischief and distracting their parents from their work. Once they took them along and kept them in the car, but the day had gotten very hot and suffocating and the children had even gotten sick. From then on they decided to leave them at home instead, although, sure enough, they worried about them all day long. Instead of packing a lunch, they would go home at noon to eat and that way they could check on them to see if they were all right. That following Monday they got up before dawn as usual and left for work. They left the children fast asleep.

"You look real happy, viejo."

"You know why."

"No, it's not just that. You look like you're happier than just because of that."

"It's just that I love my children so much, like you. And on the way I was thinking about how they also like to play with us."

At about ten o'clock that morning, from where they were working in the fields they noticed smoke rising from the direction of the farm. Everyone stopped working and ran to their cars. They sped toward the farm. When they arrived they found the Garcías' shack engulfed in flames. Only the eldest child was saved. The bodies of the other children were charred in the blaze.

"They say that the oldest child made little Juan and María put on the gloves. They were just playing. But then I think he rubbed some alcohol on their chests and who knows what other stuff on their little bodies like they had seen done in the movie. That's how they were playing."

"But how did the fire get started?"

"Well, poor things, the oldest, Raulito, started to fry some eggs while they were playing and somehow or other their little bodies caught on fire, and you can imagine."

"He must have rubbed lots of alcohol on them."

"You know all the junk that piles up in the house, so cramped for space and all. I believe the kerosene tank on the stove exploded and . . . that was it. The explosion must have covered them with flames and, of course, the shack, too."

"Why, sure."

"And you know what?"

"What?"

"The only thing that didn't get burnt up was the pair of gloves. They say they found the little girl all burnt up and with the gloves on."

"But I wonder why the gloves didn't get burned up?"

"Well, you know how those people can make things so good. Not even fire can destroy them."

"And the Garcías, how are they getting along?"

"Well, they're getting over their grief,

although I don't believe they'll ever be able to forget it. What else can you do? I tell you, you never know when your turn's up. My heart goes out to them. But you never know."

"So true."

It was a beautiful wedding day. Throughout the entire week prior the groom and his father had been busy fixing up the yard at the bride's house and setting up a canvas tent where the couple would receive the congratulations of family and friends. For decorations they used the limbs of pecan trees and wild flowers and everything was arranged very nicely. Then they smoothed down the ground in front of the tent very neatly. Every little while they sprinkled water on it to pack down the soil. This way the dust wouldn't get stirred up so much once the dancing got started. After they were married in the church the couple strolled down the street followed by a procession of godmothers and godfathers and ahead of them a bunch of children running and shouting, "Here come the newlyweds!"

The Night the Lights Went Out

〜

The night the lights of the town went out some became frightened and others did not. It wasn't storming nor was there any lightning, so some didn't find out until later. Those who were at the dance had found out but those who weren't hadn't . . . until the next day. Those who stayed home just noticed that right after the lights went out the music was no longer heard through the night and they figured that the dance had ended. But they didn't find out anything until the next day.

"That Ramón, he loved his girlfriend a lot. Yes, he loved her a lot. I know so because he was my friend and, well, you know he wasn't one who talked much, but anyway, he would tell me everything. Many times he'd say how much he loved her. They'd been going together since last year and they had given each other real pretty rings that they bought at Kress. And she loved him too but who knows what had happened this summer. They say it was the first time in four months that he had seen her . . . no one knows, no one really knows . . ."

"Look, I promise you I'm not gonna see anybody else or flirt with anyone. I promise you. I want to marry you . . . Look, we can go away together right now if you want to . . . Well, we'll wait then, until we finish school. But, look, I promise you I won't go around with anyone else nor flirt with anyone. I promise you. We can leave right now if you want to. I can support you. I know, I know . . . but they'll get over it. Let's go. Will you go with me?"

"No, it's better to wait, don't you think? It's better if we do it right. I promise you too . . . You know that I love you. Trust me. Dad wants me to finish school. And, well, I have to do what he says. But that doesn't mean I don't love you just 'cause I can't go away with you. I do love you, I love you very much. I won't go around with anybody else either. I promise you."

"Oh, come on. You know everybody knows. I heard something else. Somebody told me that she'd been going around with some dude out there in Minnesota. And that she still kept on writing to Ramón. Kept on lying to him. Some of Ramón's friends told him everything. They were working at the same farm where she was. And then when they saw him out here they told him right off. He was faithful to her but she wasn't. She was going around with some guy from San Antonio. He was nothing but a show-off and he was always all duded up. They say he wore orange shoes and real long coats and always had his collar turned up . . . But her, I think she liked to mess around, otherwise she wouldn't have been unfaithful. What was bad was her not breaking up with him. When he found out, Juanita hadn't returned yet from up north and he took to drinking a lot. I saw him once when he was drunk and all he would say was that he was hurting. That that was all that women left behind, nothing but pain inside."

"When I get back to Texas I'll take her away with me. I can't go on like this anymore. She'll come with me. She will. She's done me wrong.

How I love her. With each swing of this hoe I hear her name. How come you feel this way when you're in love? I no sooner finish supper and I'm staring at her picture until dark. And at noon, during the lunch hour, too. But the thing is, I don't really remember how she looks. The picture doesn't seem to look like her anymore. Or she doesn't look like the picture. When the others make fun of me, I just go off to the woods. I see the picture but I just don't remember anymore how she looks, even if I see her picture. Maybe it's best to not look at it so much. She promised she'd be faithful. And she is, because her eyes and her smile keep telling me so when I picture her in my mind. Soon it'll be time to return to Texas. Each time I wake to the early crow of the roosters I feel like I'm already there and that I'm watching her walk down the street. It won't be long now."

"Well, it's not that I don't love Ramón, but this guy, he's a real smooth talker and we just talk, that's all. And all the girls just stare at him. He dresses really fine, too. It's not that I don't love Ramón, but this guy is real nice and his smile, I see it all day long . . . No, I'm not breaking up with Ramón. And, anyway, what's wrong with just talking? I don't want to get serious with this guy, I promised Ramón . . . but he just keeps on following and following me around. I don't want to get serious with him . . . I don't want to lose Ramón, I'm not getting involved with this guy. I just want him around to make the other girls jealous. No, I can't break up with Ramón because I really do love him a lot. It won't be long before we'll see each other again . . . Who said he was talking to Petra? Well, then, why is he always following me around? I'll have you know he even sends me letters every day with Don José's little boy."

". . . I know you're going with someone else but I like talking to you. Since I got here and saw you I want to be with you more and more. Go to the dance Saturday and dance with me all night . . . Love you, Ramiro."

"They say she danced the whole night with Ramiro. I think her friends told her something about it but she just ignored them. This happened about the time when the work season was almost over and at the last dance, when they were saying good-bye, they promised to see each other back here. I don't think she even remembered Ramón at that moment. But by then Ramón already knew everything. That's why on that day, after not seeing each other in four months, he threw it all in her face. I was with him that day, I was with him when he saw her and I remember well that he was so happy to see her that he wasn't mad anymore. But then, after talking to her for a while he started getting mad all over again. They broke up right then and there."

"You do whatever you want."
"You can be sure of that."
"You're breaking up with me?"
"Yeah, and if you go to the dance tonight you better not dance with anyone else."
"And why shouldn't I? We're not going around anymore. We broke up. You can't tell me what to do."

"I don't care if we broke up or not. You're gonna pay for this. You're gonna do what I say, when I say and for as long as I say. Nobody makes a fool out of me. You're gonna pay for this one, one way or another."

"You can't tell me what to do."

"You're gonna do what I say and if you don't dance with me, you don't dance with anyone. And I mean for the entire dance."

"Well, they say that Juanita asked her parents for permission to leave early for the dance. She went with some of her friends and the orchestra hadn't even started playing yet and there they were already at the dance hall, standing by the door so the guys would see them and ask them to dance right away. Juanita had been dancing with only one guy when Ramón got there. He walked in and looked all around for her. He saw her dancing and when the song ended he went over and grabbed her away from the guy. This guy, just a kid, didn't say anything, he just walked away and asked someone else to dance. Anyway, when the music started again Juanita refused to dance with Ramón. They were standing right in the middle of the dance floor and all the other couples were dancing around them. They stood there arguing and then she slapped him, and he yelled something at her and charged out of the dance hall. Juanita walked over to a bench and sat down. The song hadn't even ended when all the lights went out. There was a bunch of yelling and screaming and they tried to turn them back on but then they saw that the whole town had blacked out."

The workers from the light company found Ramón inside the power plant that was about a block away from the dance hall. They say that his body was burnt to a crisp and that he was holding on to one of the transformers. That's why all the lights of the town went out. The people at the dance found out almost right away. And the ones who were close to Ramón and Juanita heard him tell her that he was going to kill himself because of her. The people at home didn't find out until the next day, that Sunday morning before and after mass.

"They just loved each other so much, don't you think?"
"No doubt."

A little before six, just before the spinach pickers would be getting home, there was the high-pitched signal of the horn at the water tank, then the sound of fire trucks, and then some moments later the ambulance sirens. By six o'clock some of the workers arrived with the news of how one of the trucks transporting workers had collided with a car and was still burning. When the car hit it, those who were not thrown out of the van on impact were trapped. Those who witnessed the crash said that the truck had immediately burst into flames and that they had seen some victims, poor souls, running from the wreckage toward the thicket with their hair aflame. They say the Anglo woman driving the car was from a dry county and that she'd been at a bar drinking, upset because her husband had left her. There were sixteen dead.

The Night Before Christmas

〜

Christmas Eve was approaching and the barrage of commercials, music and Christmas cheer over the radio and the blare of announcements over the loud speakers on top of the station wagon advertising movies at the Teatro Ideal resounded and seemed to draw it closer. It was three days before Christmas when Doña María decided to buy something for her children. This was the first time she would buy them toys. Every year she intended to do it but she always ended up facing up to the fact that, no, they couldn't afford it. She knew that her husband would be bringing each of the children candies and nuts anyway and, so she would rationalize that they didn't need to get them anything else. Nevertheless, every Christmas the children asked for toys. She always appeased them with the same promise. She would tell them to wait until the sixth of January, the day of the Magi, and by the time that day arrived the children had already forgotten all about it. But now she was noticing that each year the children seemed less and less taken with Don Chon's visit on Christmas Eve when he came bearing a sack of oranges and nuts.

"But why doesn't Santa Claus bring us anything?"

"What do you mean? What about the oranges and nuts he brings you?"

"No, that's Don Chon."

"No, I'm talking about what you always find under the sewing machine."

"What, Dad's the one who brings that, don't think we don't know that. Aren't we good like the other kids?"

"Of course, you're good children. Why don't

you wait until the day of the Reyes Magos. That's when toys and gifts really arrive. In Mexico, it's not Santa Claus who brings gifts, but the Three Wise men. And they don't come until the sixth of January. That's the real date."

"Yeah, but they always forget. They've never brought us anything, not on Christmas Eve, not on the day of the Three Kings."

"Well, maybe this time they will."

"Yeah, well, I sure hope so."

That was why she made up her mind to buy them something. But they didn't have the money to spend on toys. Her husband worked almost eighteen hours a day washing dishes and cooking at a restaurant. He didn't have time to go downtown and buy toys. Besides, they had to save money every week to pay for the trip up north. Now they even charged for children too, even if they rode standing up the whole way to Iowa. So it cost them a lot to make the trip. In any case, that night when her husband arrived, tired from work, she talked to him about getting something for the children.

"Look, viejo, the children want something for Christmas."

"What about the oranges and nuts I bring them."

"Well, they want toys. They're not content anymore with just fruits and nuts. They're a little older now and more aware of things."

"They don't need anything."

"Now, you can't tell me you didn't have toys when you were a kid."

"I used to *make* my own toys, out of clay . . . little horses and little soldiers . . ."

"Yes, but it's different here. They see so many

things . . . come on, let's go get them something
. . . I'll go to Kress myself."

"You?"

"Yes, me."

"Aren't you afraid to go downtown? You
remember that time in Wilmar, out in Minnesota,
how you got lost downtown. Are you sure you're
not afraid?"

"Yes, yes, I remember, but I'll just have to get
my courage up. I've thought about it all day long
and I've set my mind to it. I'm sure I won't get
lost here. Look, I go out to the street. From here
you can see the ice house. It's only four blocks
away, so Doña Regina tells me. When I get to the
ice house I turn to the right and go two blocks
and there's downtown. Kress is right there. Then,
I come out of Kress, walk back towards the ice
house and turn back on this street, and here I
am."

"I guess it really won't be difficult. Yeah.
Fine. I'll leave you some money on top of the
table when I go to work in the morning. But be
careful, vieja, there's a lot of people downtown
these days."

The fact was that Doña María very rarely left the
house. The only time she did was when she visited her
father and her sister who lived on the next block. And
she only went to church whenever someone died and,
occasionally, when there was a wedding. But she went
with her husband, so she never took notice of where
she was going. And her husband always brought her
everything. He was the one who bought the groceries
and clothing. In reality she was unfamiliar with
downtown even though it was only six blocks away.
The cemetery was on the other side of downtown and
the church was also in that direction. The only time

that they passed through downtown was whenever they were on their way to San Antonio or whenever they were returning from up north. And this would usually be during the wee hours of the morning or at night. But that day she was determined and she started making preparations.

The next day she got up early as usual, and after seeing her husband and children off, she took the money from the table and began getting ready to go downtown. This didn't take her long.

> "My God, I don't know why I'm so fearful. Why, downtown is only six blocks from here. I just go straight and then after I cross the tracks turn right. Then go two blocks and there's Kress. On the way back, I walk two blocks back and then I turn to the left and keep walking until I'm home again. God willing, there won't be any dogs on the way. And I just pray that the train doesn't come while I'm crossing the tracks and catches me right in the middle . . . I just hope there's no dogs . . . I hope there's no train coming down the tracks."

She walked the distance from the house to the railroad tracks rapidly. She walked down the middle of the street all the way. She was afraid to walk on the sidewalk. She feared she might get bitten by a dog or that someone might grab her. In actuality there was only one dog along the entire stretch and most of the people didn't even notice her walking toward downtown. She nevertheless kept walking down the middle of the street and, luckily, not a single car passed by, otherwise she would not have known what to do. Upon arriving at the crossing she was suddenly struck by intense fear. She could hear the sound of moving trains and their whistles blowing and this was unnerving her. She was too scared to cross. Each time she mustered enough courage to cross she heard the whistle of the train and, frightened, she retreated and ended up at the same place. Finally, overcoming her fear, she shut her eyes and crossed the tracks. Once she got past the tracks, her fear began to subside. She got to the corner and turned to the right.

The sidewalks were crowded with people and her ears started to fill up with a ringing sound, the kind that, once it started, it wouldn't stop. She didn't recognize any of the people around her. She wanted to turn back but she was caught in the flow of the crowd which shoved her onward toward downtown and the sound kept ringing louder and louder in her ears. She became frightened and more and more she was finding herself unable to remember why she was there amidst the crowd of people. She stopped in an alley way between two stores to regain her composure a bit. She stood there for a while watching the passing crowd.

"My God, what is happening to me? I'm starting to feel the same way I did in Wilmar. I hope I don't get worse. Let me see . . . the ice house is in that direction—no it's that way. No, my God, what's happening to me? Let me see . . . I came from over there to here. So it's in that direction. I should have just stayed home. Uh, can you tell me where Kress is, please? . . . Thank you."

She walked to where they had pointed and entered the store. The noise and pushing of the crowd was worse inside. Her anxiety soared. All she wanted was to leave the store but she couldn't find the doors anywhere, only stacks and stacks of merchandise and people crowded against one another. She even started hearing voices coming from the merchandise. For a while she stood, gazing blankly at what was in front of her. She couldn't even remember the names of the things. Some people stared at her for a few seconds, others just pushed her aside. She remained in this state for a while, then she started walking again. She finally made out some toys and put them in her bag. Then she saw a wallet and also put that in her bag. Suddenly she no longer heard the noise of the crowd. She only saw the people moving about—their legs, their arms, their mouths, their eyes. She finally asked where the door, the exit was. They told her and she started in that direction. She pressed through the crowd, pushing her way until she pushed open the door and exited.

She had been standing on the sidewalk for only a few seconds, trying to figure out where she was, when she felt someone grab her roughly by the arm. She was grabbed so tightly that she gave out a cry.

"Here she is . . . these damn people, always stealing something, stealing. I've been watching you all along. Let's have that bag."
"But . . ."

Then she heard nothing for a long time. All she saw was the pavement moving swiftly toward her face and a small pebble that bounced into her eye and was hurting a lot. She felt someone pulling her arms and when they turned her, face up, all she saw were faces far away. Then she saw a security guard with a gun in his holster and she was terrified. In that instant she thought about her children and her eyes filled with tears. She started crying. Then she lost consciousness of what was happening around her, only feeling herself drifting in a sea of people, their arms brushing against her like waves.

"It's a good thing my compadre happened to be there. He's the one who ran to the restaurant to tell me. How do you feel?"

"I think I must be insane, viejo."

"That's why I asked you if you weren't afraid you might get sick like in Wilmar."

"What will become of my children with a mother who's insane? A crazy woman who can't even talk, can't even go downtown."

"Anyway, I went and got the notary public. He's the one who went with me to the jail. He explained everything to the official. That you got dizzy and that you get nervous attacks whenever you're in a crowd of people."

"And if they send me to the insane asylum? I don't want to leave my children. Please, viejo, don't let them take me, don't let them. I shouldn't have gone downtown."

"Just stay here inside the house and don't leave the yard. There's no need for it anyway. I'll bring you everything you need. Look, don't cry anymore, don't cry. No, go ahead and cry, it'll make you feel better. I'm gonna talk to the kids and tell them to stop bothering you about Santa Claus. I'm gonna tell them there's no Santa Claus, that way they won't trouble you with that anymore."

"No, viejo, don't be mean. Tell them that if he doesn't bring them anything on Christmas Eve, it's because the Reyes Magos will be bringing them something."

"But . . . well, all right, whatever you say. I suppose it's always best to have hope."

The children, who were hiding behind the door, heard everything, but they didn't quite understand it all. They awaited the day of the Reyes Magos as they did every year. When that day came and went with no arrival of gifts, they didn't ask for explanations.

Before people left for up north the priest would bless their cars and trucks at five dollars each. One time he made enough money to take a trip to Barcelona, in Spain, to visit his parents and friends. He brought back words of gratitude from his family and some postcards of a very modern church. These he placed by the entrance of the church for the people to see, that they might desire a church such as that one. It wasn't long before words began to appear on the cards, then crosses, lines, and con safos symbols, just as had happened to the new church pews. The priest was never able to understand the sacrilege.

The Portrait

~

As soon as the people returned from up north the portrait salesmen began arriving from San Antonio. They would come to rake in. They knew that the workers had money and that was why, as Dad used to say, they would flock in. They carried suitcases packed with samples and always wore white shirts and ties. That way they looked more important and the people believed everything they would tell them and invite them into their homes without giving it much thought. I think that down deep they even longed for their children to one day be like them. In any event, they would arrive and make their way down the dusty streets, going house to house carrying suitcases full of samples.

I remember once I was at the house of one of my father's friends when one of these salesmen arrived. I also remember that that particular one seemed a little frightened and timid. Don Mateo asked him to come in because he wanted to do business.

"Good afternoon, traveler. I would like to tell you about something new that we're offering this year."

"Well, let's see, let's see . . ."

"Well, sir, see, you give us a picture, any picture you may have, and we will not only enlarge it for you but we'll also set it in a wooden frame like this one and with inlays, like this— three dimensional, as they say."

"And what for?"

"So that it will look real. That way . . . look, let me show you . . . see? Doesn't he look real, like he's alive?"

"Man, he sure does. Look, vieja. This looks

great. Well, you know, we wanted to send some pictures to be enlarged . . . but now, this must cost a lot, right?"

"No, I'll tell you, it costs about the same. Of course, it takes more time."

"Well, tell me, how much?"

"For as little as thirty dollars we'll deliver it to you done with inlays just like this, one this size."

"Boy, that's expensive! Didn't you say it didn't cost a lot more? Do you take installments?"

"Well, I'll tell you, we have a new manager and he wants everything in cash. It's very fine work. We'll make it look like real. Done like that, with inlays . . . take a look. What do you think? Some fine work, wouldn't you say? We can have it all finished for you in a month. You just tell us what color you want the clothes to be and we'll come by with it all finished one day when you least expect, framed and all. Yes, sir, a month at the longest. But like I say, this man who's the new manager, he wants the full payment in cash. He's very demanding, even with us."

"Yes, but it's much too expensive."

"Well, yes. But the thing is, this is very fine work. You can't say you've ever seen portraits done like this, with wood inlays."

"No, well, that's true. What do you think, vieja?"

"Well, I like it a lot. Why don't we order one? And if it turns out good . . . my Chuy . . . may he rest in peace. It's the only picture we have of him. We took it right before he left for Korea. Poor m'ijo, we never saw him again. See . . . this is his picture. Do you think you can make it like that, make it look like he's alive?"

"Sure, we can. You know, we've done a lot of them in soldier's uniforms and shaped it, like you see in this sample, with inlays. Why, it's more than just a portrait. Sure. You just tell me what size you want and whether you want a round or square frame. What do you say? How should I write it down?"

"What do you say, vieja, should we have it done like this one?"

"Well, I've already told you what I think. I would like to have m'ijo's picture fixed up like that and in color."

"All right, go ahead and write it down. But you take good care of that picture for us because it's the only one we have of our son grown up. He was going to send us one all dressed up in uniform with the American and Mexican flags crossed over his head, but he no sooner got there when a letter arrived telling us that he was lost in action. So you take good care of it."

"Don't you worry. We're responsible people. And we understand the sacrifices that you people make. Don't worry. And you just wait and see. When we bring it to you you'll see how pretty it's gonna look. What do you say, should we make the uniform navy blue?"

"But he's not wearing a uniform in that picture."

"No, but that's just a matter of fixing it up with some wood fiber overlays. Look at these. This one, he didn't have a uniform on but we put one on him. So what do you say? Should we make it navy blue?"

"All right."

"Don't you worry about the picture."

And that was how they spent the entire day going house to house, street by street, their suitcases stuffed with pictures. As it turned out, a whole lot of people had ordered enlargements of that kind.

"They should be delivering those portraits soon, don't you think?"

"I think so, it's delicate work and takes more time. That's some fine work those people do. Did you see how real those pictures looked?"

"Yeah, sure. They do some fine work. You can't deny that. But it's already been over a month since they passed by here."

"Yes, but from here they went on through all the towns picking up pictures . . . all the way to San Antonio for sure. So it'll probably take a little longer."

"That's true, that's true."

And two more weeks had passed by the time they made the discovery. Some very heavy rains had come and some children who were playing in one of the tunnels leading to the dump found a sack full of pictures, all worm-eaten and soaking wet. The only reason they could tell that these were pictures was because there were a lot of them and most of them the same size and with faces that could just barely be made out. Everybody caught on right away. Don Mateo was so angry that he took off to San Antonio to find the so and so who had swindled them.

"Well, you know, I stayed at Esteban's house. And every day I went with him to the market to sell produce. I helped him with everything. I had faith that I would run into that son of a gun some day soon. Then, after I'd been there for a few days, I started going out to the different barrios and I found out a lot that way. It wasn't so much the money that upset me. It was my poor vieja, crying and all because we'd lost the only picture we had of Chuy. We found it in the sack with all the other pictures but it was already ruined, you know."

"I see, but tell me, how did you find him?"

"Well, you see, to make a long story short, he came by the stand at the market one day. He stood right in front of us and bought some vegetables. It was like he was trying to remember who I was. Of course, I recognized him right off. Because when you're angry enough, you don't forget a face. I just grabbed him right then and there. Poor guy couldn't even talk. He was all scared. And I told him that I wanted that portrait of my son and that I wanted it three dimensional and that he'd best get it for me or I'd let him have it. And I went with him to where he lived. And I put him to work right then and there. The poor guy didn't know where to begin. He had to do it all from memory."

"And how did he do it?"

"I don't know. I suppose if you're scared enough, you're capable of doing anything. Three days later he brought me the portrait all finished, just like you see it there on that table by the Virgin Mary. Now tell me, how do you like the way my boy looks?"

"Well, to be honest, I don't remember too well how Chuy looked. But he was beginning to look more and more like you, isn't that so?"

"Yes, I would say so. That's what everybody tells me now. That Chuy's a chip off the old block and that he was already looking like me. There's the portrait. Like they say, one and the same."

"They let Figueroa out. He's been out a week."

"Yeah, but he's not well. There in the pen, if they don't like someone, they'll give them injections so they'll die."

"Damn right. Who do you think turned him in?"

"Probably some gringo who couldn't stand seeing him in town with that white girl he brought back with him from Wisconsin. And no one to defend him. They say the little gringa was seventeen and it's against the law."

"I'll bet you he won't last a year."

"Well, they say he has a very strange disease."

When We Arrive

~

At about four o'clock in the morning the truck broke down. All night they stood hypnotized by the high-pitched whir of the tires turning against the pavement. When the truck stopped they awakened. The silence alone told them something was wrong. All along the way the truck had been overheating and then when they stopped and checked the motor they saw that it had practically burned up. It just wouldn't go anymore. They would have to wait there until daybreak and then ask for a lift to the next town. Inside the trailer the people awakened and then struck up several conversations. Then in the darkness their eyes had gradually begun to close and all became so silent that all that could be heard was the chirping of the crickets. Some were sleeping, others were thinking.

"Good thing the truck stopped here. My stomach's been hurting a lot for some time but I would've had to wake up a lot of people to get to the window and ask them to stop. But you still can't hardly see anything. Well, I'm getting off, see if I can find a field or a ditch. Must've been that chile I ate, it was so hot but I hated to let it go to waste. I hope my vieja is doing all right in there, carrying the baby and all."

"This driver that we have this year is a good one. He keeps on going. He doesn't stop for anything. Just gases up and let's go. We've been on the road over twenty-four hours. We should be close to Des Moines. Sure wish I could sit down for just a little while at least. I'd get out and lie down on the side of the road but there's no telling if there's snakes or some other kind of animal.

Just before I fell asleep on my feet it felt like my knees were going to buckle. But I guess your body gets used to it right away 'cause it doesn't seem so hard anymore. But the kids must feel real tired standing like this all the way and with nothing to hold on to. Us grownups can at least hold on to this center bar that supports the canvas. And to think we're not as crowded as other times. I think there must be forty of us at the most. I remember that one time I traveled with that bunch of wetbacks, there were more than sixty of us. We couldn't even smoke."

"What a stupid woman! How could she be so dumb as to throw that diaper out the front of the truck. It came sliding along the canvas and good thing I had glasses on or I would even have gotten the shit in my eyes! What a stupid woman! How could she do that? She should've known that crap would be blown towards all of us standing up back here. Why the hell couldn't she just wait until we got to a gas station and dump the shit there!"

"El Negrito just stood there in disbelief when I ordered the fifty-four hamburgers. At two in the morning. And since I walked into the restaurant alone and I'm sure he didn't see the truck pull up loaded with people. His eyes just popped wide open . . . 'at two o'clock in the morning, hamburgers? Fifty-four of them? Man, you must eat one hell of a lot.' It's that the people hadn't eaten and the driver asked for just one of us to get out and order for everyone. El Negrito was astounded. He couldn't believe what I ordered, that I wanted fifty-four hamburgers. At two o'clock in the morning you can eat that many hamburgers very easily, especially when you're starving."

"This is the last fuckin' year I come out here. As soon as we get to the farm I'm getting the hell out. I'll go look for a job in Minneapolis. I'll be damned if I go back to Texas. Out here you can at least make a living at a decent job. I'll look for my uncle, see if he can find me a job at the hotel where he works as a bellboy. Who knows, maybe they'll give me a break there or at some other hotel. And then the gringas, that's just a matter of finding them."

"If things go well this year, maybe we'll buy us a car so we won't have to travel this way, like cattle. The girls are pretty big now and I know they feel embarrassed. Sometimes they have some good buys at the gas stations out there. I'll talk to my compadre, he knows some of the car salesmen. I'll get one I like, even if it's old. I'm tired of coming out here in a truck like this. My compadre drove back a good little car last year. If we do well with the onion crop, I'll buy me one that's at least half-way decent. I'll teach my boy how to drive and he can take it all the way to Texas. As long as he doesn't get lost like my nephew. They didn't stop to ask for directions and ended up in New Mexico instead of Texas. Or I'll get Mundo to drive it and I won't charge him for gas. I'll see if he wants to."

"With the money Mr. Thompson loaned me we have enough to buy food for at least two months. By then we should have the money from the beet crop. Just hope we don't get too much in debt. He loaned me two-hundred dollars but by the time you pay for the trip practically half of it is gone, and now that they've started charging me half-fare for the children . . . And then when we return, I have to pay him back double. Four-hundred dollars. That's too much interest, but what can you do? When you need it, you need it. Some people have told me to report him because that's way too much interest but now he's even got the deed to the house. I'm just hoping that things go okay for us with the beet crop or else we'll be left to the wind, homeless. We have to save enough to pay him back the four hundred. And then we'll see if we have something left. And these kids, they need to start going to school. I don't know. I hope it goes okay for us, if not I don't know how we're going to do it. I just pray to God that there's work."

"Fuckin' life, this goddamn fuckin' life! This fuckin' sonofabitchin' life for being pendejo! pendejo! pendejo! We're nothing but a bunch of stupid, goddamn asses! To hell with this goddamn motherfuckin' life! This is the last time I go through this, standing up all the way like a goddamn animal. As soon as we get there I'm headed for Minneapolis. Somehow I'll find me something to do where I don't have to work like a fuckin' mule. Fuckin' life! One of these days they'll fuckin' pay for this. Sonofabitch! I'll be goddamn for being such a fuckin' pendejo!"

"Poor viejo. He must be real tired now, standing up the whole trip. I saw him nodding off a little while ago. And with no way to help him, what with these two in my arms. How I wish we were there already so we could lie down, even if it's on the hard floor. These children are nothing but trouble. I hope I'll be able to help him out in the fields, but I'm afraid that this year, what with these kids, I won't be able to do anything. I have to breastfeed them every little while and then they're still so little. If only they were just a bit older. I'm still going to try my best to help him out. At least along his row so he won't feel so overworked. Even if it's just for short whiles. My poor viejo . . . the children are still so little and already he wishes they could start school. I just hope I'll be able to help him. God willing, I'll be able to help him."

"What a great view of the stars from here! It looks like they're coming down and touching the tarp of the truck. It's almost like there aren't any people inside. There's hardly any traffic at this hour. Every now and then a trailer passes by. The silence of the morning twilight makes everything look like it's made of satin. And now, what do I wipe myself with? Why couldn't it always be early dawn like this? We're going to be here till midday for sure. By the time they find help in the town and then by the time they fix the motor . . . If only it could stay like early dawn, then nobody would complain. I'm going to keep my eyes on the stars till the last one disappears. I wonder how many more people are watching the same star? And how many more might there be wondering how many are looking at the same star? It's so silent it looks like it's the stars the crickets are calling to."

"Goddamn truck. It's nothing but trouble. When we get there everybody will just have to look out for themselves. All I'm doing is dropping them off with the growers and I'm getting the hell out. Besides, we don't have a contract. They'll find themselves somebody to take them back to Texas. Somebody's bound to come by and pick them up. You can't make money off beets anymore. My best bet is to head back to Texas just as soon as I drop these people off and then see how things go hauling watermelons. The melon season's almost here. All I need now is for there not to be anyone in this goddamn town who can fix the truck. What the hell will I do then? So long as the cops don't come by and start hassling me about moving the truck from here. Boy, that town had to be the worst. We didn't even stop and still the cop caught up with us just to tell us that he didn't want us staying there. I guess he just wanted to show off in front of the town people. But we didn't even stop in their goddamn town. When we get there, as soon as I drop them off, I'll turn back. Each one to fend for himself."

"When we get there I'm gonna see about getting a good bed for my vieja. Her kidneys are really bothering her a lot nowadays. Just hope we don't end up in a chicken coop like last year, with that cement floor. Even though you cover it with straw, once the cold season sets in you just can't stand it. That was why my rheumatism got so bad, I'm sure of that."

"When we arrive, when we arrive, the real truth is that I'm tired of arriving. Arriving and leaving, it's the same thing because we no sooner arrive and . . . the real truth of the matter . . . I'm tired of arriving. I really should say when we don't arrive because that's the real truth. We never arrive."

"When we arrive, when we arrive . . ."

Little by little the crickets ceased their chirping. It seemed as though they were becoming tired and the dawn gradually affirmed the presence of objects, ever so carefully and very slowly, so that no one would take notice of what was happening. And the people were becoming people. They began getting out of the trailer and they huddled around and commenced to talk about what they would do when they arrived.

Bartolo passed through town every December when he knew that most of the people had returned from work up north. He always came by selling his poems. By the end of the first day, they were almost sold out because the names of the people of the town appeared in the poems. And when he read them aloud it was something emotional and serious. I recall that one time he told the people to read the poems out loud because the spoken word was the seed of love in the darkness.

Under the House

~~~

The fleas made him move. He was under a house. He had been there for several hours, or so it seemed to him, hiding. That morning on his way to school he felt the urge not to go. He thought of how the teacher would spank him for sure because he didn't know the words. Then he thought of crawling under the house but not just because of that. He felt like hiding, too, but he didn't know where nor for how long, so he just went ahead and hid there. At first the fleas didn't bother him and he felt very comfortable in the dark. Although he was sure there were spiders, he had crawled in unafraid and there he remained. From where he was all he could make out was a white strip of daylight, about a foot high, lining the house all around. He was lying face down and whenever he moved he could feel his back brush against the floor of the house. This even gave him a feeling of security. But once the fleas started biting him he had to move constantly. And he started to worry that the people who lived there might find out that he was there and make him get out. But he had to keep moving constantly.

I wonder how long I've been here now. The kids came out of the house to play some time ago. It seems I've been here for a good while. As long as they don't look under the house 'cause they'll see me for sure, and then what? The children look funny, all I can see are their legs running. It's not bad here. I could come here every day. I think that must be what the others do when they play hooky. No one to bother me here. I can think in peace.

He had even forgotten all about the fleas and even that he was under the house. He could think very clearly in the dark. He didn't need to close his eyes. He thought about his father for a while, about how he used to tell him stories at night about witches and how he would make them fall from the sky by praying and tying the seven knots.

When I'd be coming back from work, at that time we had our own land with irrigation, in the early morning twilight, I'd always see these globes of light, like fireballs, bouncing off the telephone lines. They would come from the direction of Morelos, they say that's where they originate. One time I nearly made one fall down. Don Remigio taught me how to say the seven prayers that go with the seven knots. All you have to do is start praying when you see those balls of fire. After each prayer you tie a knot. This one time I got to the seventh prayer but you know, I wasn't able to tie that last knot, but the witch fell anyway, practically landing at my feet, and then she got up . . . The boy was so young and children don't understand too much at that age. And he couldn't hold out. They're not going to do anything to the boss, he's got too much pull. Can you imagine what they'd do if one of us killed one of their kids? They say that one day the boy's father took a rifle and went looking for him because he wanted to pay him back but he didn't find him . . . The woman would almost always start crying when she entered the church, and then she'd start praying. But before she was even aware of it, she would start talking in a loud voice. Then she'd start yelling, like she was having some kind of attack . . . I think Doña Cuquita is still living. I haven't seen her in a long time. She used to be very careful whenever we went to the dump. Now her I really loved. And since I never knew my grandparents. I think even Dad loved her like a grandmother because he, too, never knew his grandparents. What I liked best was for her to embrace me and tell me, "You're smarter than an eagle and more watchful than the moon" . . . Get out of there! Get away from that goddamn window! Go away! Go away . . . You know, you can't come home with me anymore. Look, I don't mind playing with you but some old ladies told mama that Mexicans steal and now mama says not to bring you home anymore. You have to turn back. But we can still play at school. I'll choose you and you choose me . . . What can I tell you! I know what I'm telling you, I'm saying that we can't get any more screwed than we already are. I know why I'm telling you. If there's another war, we won't be the ones to suffer. Don't be a damn fool. The ones who will pay for it are the ones on top, the ones who have something. Us, we're already screwed. If there's another war, hell, things might even get better for us . . . Why don't you eat sweet bread anymore? You don't like it, anymore? . . . Well, I tell you, I even went downtown and bought me a new hammer so I could be ready for when they'd come to teach us. They say that the minister, when he found out, he went straight home, took a hatchet and broke all the furniture to pieces and then he took everything outside and set it on fire. He stood there and watched everything burn to ashes . . . I don't think my viejo is going to be able to work out in the sun anymore. The boss didn't say a thing when we told him that he had gotten sick from the heat. He just shook his head. What worried him the most was that it was raining too much and the crop was getting ruined. That was the only thing he was sad about. He wasn't even sad when they had to operate on his wife because she had cancer, much less when we told him about my viejo . . . These sonofabitches are gonna cut your hair, I'll see to that, if I have to bust their noses . . . There is no devil, there isn't. The only devil is Don Rayos when he dresses up with horns and with the cape to go to the shepherd's play . . . Goddamn fool! Why don't you pay attention to what you're doing? You almost crashed with that truck! Didn't you see it? Are you blind, or what? . . . Why did the teacher cry when they came for him? Ever since he was put in her class she always just kept looking at him. And she was so young, she wasn't like the ones in Texas, little old ladies holding a paddle in their hands making sure you didn't lose your place in the book. And if you did, pow! They'd just bend you over . . . You think that was how they were burned? It's just hard to believe. But so fast? It's that fire spreads fast and once your clothes catch on fire, that's it. You remember that family that died in that fire around Christmas time? They fell asleep, never to wake up again. And then the firemen crying as they removed the bodies, the grease from the children's little burned up bodies dripping all over their boots . . . Free citizens, this is a day of magnificent and profound importance. It was in the year eighteen hundred and seventy-two that Napoleon's troops suffered a defeat against Mexican soldiers who fought so valiantly—that was how I would begin my discourse. I always used the words "free citizens" when I was young, son, but now ever since I had the attack I can't remember too well

*anymore what I would say to the people. Then
came the Revolution and in the end we lost. Villa
made out well but I had to come out here. No
one here knows what I went through. Sometimes
I want to remember but, truth is, I'm not able to
anymore. All my thoughts become hazy. Now,
tell me, what is it that you most desire at this
moment of your life? At this very moment . . .
Yesterday we collected fifty pounds of copper in
all. Enrique found a magnet and that makes it
much easier to find the iron buried under so
much junk that people throw away. Sometimes
we do well but usually it's a waste of time. But at
least enough to buy something to eat. And tell
me, what's the price of tin these days? Why don't
you all come with us next time we go? . . . The
cold weather is setting in. I'll bet you that tomorrow morning the ground will be all covered
with frost. And notice how often the cranes fly
by . . . There's going to be a wedding Sunday. For
sure they'll serve us cabrito in mole sauce, with
rice, and then the dance, and the groom, anxious
for night to arrive . . . I tell you, comadre, we got
so frightened last night when the lights went out.
We were there playing with the children when all
of a sudden it was pitch dark. And we didn't even
have one candle. But that wasn't why we got
frightened. That knucklehead, Juan, was eating
an orange and we don't know how but he got a
seed in his nose and we couldn't get it out in the
dark. And he was just crying and crying. And
your compadre, lighting match after match. I
wonder what happened. Why, all the lights of the
town went out . . . They found Doña Amada's
son in a ditch and Don Tiburcio's son inside the
trailer. I think they're going to sue Don Jesús for
transporting people in a closed van. They say*

that when they tried to stretch out his body, because they found him all curled up in a corner, when they tried to stretch him out to put him in the hearse, one of his legs fell off . . . Those people who sell those portraits don't come around here anymore. Don Mateo gave them a good scare . . . Mom nearly lost her mind. She always started crying whenever she talked with anyone about what happened to her downtown.

I would like to see all of the people together. And then, if I had great big arms, I could embrace them all. I wish I could talk to all of them again, but all of them together. But that, only in a dream. I like it right here because I can think about anything I please. Only by being alone can you bring everybody together. That's what I needed to do, hide, so that I could come to understand a lot of things. From now on, all I have to do is to come here, in the dark, and think about them. And I have so much to think about and I'm missing so many years. I think today what I wanted to do was recall this past year. And that's just one year. I'll have to come here to recall all of the other years.

He became aware of the present when he heard one of the children yelling and at the same time felt a blow to his leg. They were throwing rocks at him under the house.

"Mami, mami, there's a man under the house! Mami, mami, mami, hurry, come here, there's a man here, there's a man here!"

"Where? Where? Ah! . . . Let me get some boards and you run and get Doña Luz's dog."

And he saw countless faces and eyes looking at him. Then it grew darker under the house. The children kept throwing rocks at him and the dog kept barking while the woman was trying to poke him with some boards.

"Who could it be?"

He had to come out. Everyone was surprised that it was him. He didn't say anything to them, just walked away. And then he heard the woman say:
"That poor family. First the mother and now him. He must be losing his mind. He's losing track of the years."

Smiling, he walked down the chuckhole-ridden street leading to his house. He immediately felt happy because, as he thought over what the woman had said, he realized that in reality he hadn't lost anything. He had made a discovery. To discover and rediscover and piece things together. This to this, that to that, all with all. That was it. That was everything. He was thrilled. When he got home he went straight to the tree that was in the yard. He climbed it. He saw a palm tree on the horizon. He imagined someone perched on top, gazing across at him. He even raised one arm and waved it back and forth so that the other could see that he knew he was there.

Related Readings

CONTENTS

from Fields of Toil: A Migrant Family's Journey

by Isabel Valle

Have circumstances for migrant workers changed since the 1940s and 1950s? In a series of articles first published by the local newspaper in Walla Walla, Washington, reporter Isabel Valle wrote about one migrant family in the early 1990s. Valle lived with the Martinez family, working in the fields and traveling with them, for an entire year. What follows is an excerpt from the book made from Valle's articles.

When work is scarce, but the need for money is pressing, often there is no other choice for migrant workers but to travel about the country seeking employment. The constant relocating, never staying in one place long enough to establish roots, and the hard, manual labor that they face just to earn a minimum wage, is nearly unbearable. But this lifestyle has been followed for many years by many people.

When speaking to migrants about their lives they are quick to point out that many of their number have died working in the fields or while traveling. To some people this may sound unbelievable, but for migrant workers it is simply a way of life. For the past 35 years, Raul and Maria Elena Martinez have left their home in LaGrulla, Texas, located at the southern tip of Texas about three miles north of the Rio Grande River (the "South Texas Valley") in search of a better life. But in many instances, their expectations have been shattered.

"This isn't an easy life. We've had to live in the worst conditions. Looking and finding work is never easy and when you have children, babies, that just makes this life much harder," Maria Elena, 52, recalls.

During the years following their marriage in 1956, the Martinezes limited their search for work to Texas, where they picked cotton, oranges, and a variety of vegetables. But with droves of other families following their footsteps, the Martinezes realized that their only hope of finding more jobs and earning a little more money was to leave the state. Through communication with other migrant families they heard of work and headed to California, Illinois, Michigan, Minnesota, and Washington to try to make a living.

The hard part, they say, is never knowing what they are going to encounter along the road or at their destination. Slipping from Spanish into English, often struggling to find the right words in English, the Martinezes recall arriving in labor camps to find they have to live in chicken coops equipped with one out-door toilet for 20 people. In other cases, milk was scarce so coffee was substituted in the baby bottles. "During this time I had children so we were traveling with babies," says Maria Elena.

In early spring each year, Raul and Maria Elena load their pickup truck with personal belongings. One by one, the younger of their 13 children pile into the vehicle, ready to leave Texas and travel the country in search of work with their parents. As with most migrant families, some years their destinations are mapped out in advance, but other years they have no clue as to where they may be going.

"Move to where we can find some work," Raul

keeps repeating in Spanish. "If we don't find any there, then we'll move somewhere else."

This year, they came to Washington state to pick asparagus, one of the hardest kinds of work they say there is. Raul, 61, and Maria Elena traveled with their sons Charlie, 15, Jimmy, 10, and Billy, 7; their daughter, Doris, 20; and son Danny, 28, his wife Alicia, 26, and their two children. They arrived in Pasco, Washington, in March and picked in the fields until the last days of June. Halfway through the harvest, the work took its toll on Doris and she returned to LaGrulla.

"I felt so sorry for her. She would finish full bottles of Tylenol for her backaches and after a while [the pills] stopped taking effect," her mother recalls. Doris, a first-year student at Texas State Technical Institute, decided to work in the fields so she could earn enough money to purchase a car. She had been offered a job at a hospital in Texas, and a car was a necessity.

"But she just couldn't make it. It's hard work and they're out there killing themselves," says Maria Elena. "It's too hard to be bending over all day long. I would see many women that would stop work and cry in the middle of the fields. Doris was one of them."

Once the asparagus harvest was over, the Martinezes arrived in Walla Walla in July with hopes of working the sweet onion harvest. It is here that I join their household. Meanwhile, Danny and his family have decided to return to Texas after they too found that the work in the fields was physically demanding with very low pay. On their way home, their truck overturned near Tremonton, Utah, when Danny fell asleep behind the wheel. Fortunately, no one was seriously injured. Family members suffered only minor cuts and bruises.

Upon their arrival in Walla Walla, the Martinezes

have found that jobs in harvesting sweet onions are scarce. Raul spent every night of the first week calling and visiting farmers in hopes of getting hired. The answers were always the same: "There's no work now, call back tomorrow and maybe we'll have something." Raul paces the house wondering how he is going to earn some money. Every day that migrants do not work is a day of lost wages that are so desperately needed.

"We need to work every day because if we don't we lose a lot of money. We may not earn money every day but we do spend it every day," Raul says. There's food to be bought to feed a family of five—which includes three growing boys—gas to fill the truck, and toiletries and other necessary items.

"All of this takes money. Things are expensive and when you have only about $600, you start to panic," Maria Elena adds.

Walla Walla, Washington: Mid-Summer

Since work in the onion fields seems long in coming, Raul has decided to look for other employment. In the two weeks they have been in Walla Walla, Raul and the family have earned money doing yard work and other odd jobs in order to make ends meet. The younger children are also looking for jobs and can be found working beside their father.

"That's what we have to do when jobs in the fields are not found, we have to find work anywhere, doing anything," Maria Elena says.

Once Raul finds work, a sense of relief takes over and the expression on his face changes. Although the work he does is hard manual labor, at night he walks around the house with a great sense of accomplishment.

"I'm happy when I'm working," Raul says with a shy smile. "I like to work and I like all kinds of work." On the days that he has no luck finding employment, Raul picks up litter around the house, washes his truck, cleans inside the house, or just walks around looking for things to fix. Raul's latest work is roofing, a job he obtained through an acquaintance.

"That's the way he is, he can never just sit around, he always has to be busy," Maria Elena says. "But what really makes him happy is that he's earning some money. Right now we only have enough to buy food. We still need money for the road, and we'd like to have a little saved up for the winter, when there is no work."

Work is a major priority for the rest of the family as well. The children have found themselves bored staying at home. The two younger children pass their days bouncing a basketball around the house or playing with neighborhood children. Charlie spends his days listening to music or looking after his younger brothers. Maria Elena keeps herself very busy cooking, cleaning, washing, and looking after the house.

But once they talk about working and earning money, their spirits brighten. Maria Elena and the children have found a job picking raspberries in nearby Milton-Freewater, Oregon. Although the idea of having to start the day at 4 a.m. may not be too appealing to the children, once they are physically dragged out of bed, placed in the car, and driven to the field, they wake up and start talking about what they are going to do with the money they earn. Charlie, meanwhile, has found employment through the Walla Walla Job Training Center. He will be working at the YWCA three times a week. The days that he is not scheduled to work, he will go to the fields with the other members of the family to pick berries. The money he earns will be spent on clothes for high school this fall.

"All my family are hard workers," Raul says. "I

want them to work so they can learn about making a living."

"I want them to work in the fields so they can see how hard it is and that way they will see the importance of a good education," Maria Elena emphasizes.

Raul adds, "We stress education to our children because it's very important and no matter what state we are in, we will always send the children back to Texas to continue school, or we will enroll them in a local school."

Although the oldest children have completed their high school education and some have even gone on to get some form of technical training, their income still comes from working in the fields. "That's because there are no jobs in the [South Texas] valley. There is nothing for us there, so every year it's the same thing, travel the country looking for work," Raul says.

"I don't want my children to come looking for work anymore. I want them to have a good job in the [South Texas] valley and a good paying job, at least $6 an hour, because they have suffered enough," Maria Elena stresses. "I've lived this way all my life and I don't want the same thing for my kids."

The Martinezes hope that factories will someday employ local residents in South Texas. "If [industries] can open up factories in Mexico and other Latin American countries so they can get cheap labor, why can't they do the exact thing in the valley? We may not be able to earn a lot of money, but at least we can stay in our homes," Maria Elena says.

With the burden of traveling from place to place in search of work comes the additional frustration of packing belongings into large green garbage bags, loading trucks to full capacity where not even the smallest space is left empty, looking for affordable housing where there is at least running water and sanitary conditions, and finally, finding food to feed the family. But even with all these deplorable conditions, the Martinezes say the worst thing they must endure is looking for work.

"The hardest part of migrant living is that when your work ends there is nothing else and you're left desperately seeking some way to get money to support your family," Raul says. "That has got to be the worst feeling, not knowing where your next paycheck will come from."

The future doesn't look bright for the Martinez family for the rest of the year. Crops throughout the country have dwindled due to severe drought or freezing temperatures, and yet with every passing day an influx of migrant workers keeps traveling down the roads looking for work. At the same time, Raul would like to retire soon and Maria Elena would love to someday settle permanently in their Texas home. The children too would like to remain in Texas where they can continue going to school with their friends. But for now the days are filled with discussions of where they have heard there is a good harvest and good pay, and how long it will take to travel to such locations.

"I think we're going to continue this way of life until we get a good job somewhere in Texas," Maria Elena says.

"Or anywhere," Raul answers.

A Rude Awakening

The "way of life" which Maria Elena has described to me is anything but comfortable. Although some of my distant relatives worked in the fields many years ago, the only thing I knew about fruits and vegetables was what I saw displayed at the grocery store. Working in the fields with the Martinez family has been a rude awakening.

To begin with, I'm not a morning person, so having

to suddenly start my days at 4 a.m. did not come easy. Maria Elena and I were the first to wake up when the alarm went off. The kitchen was the first place she headed, to brew fresh coffee and prepare flour tortillas, scrambled eggs, and refried beans. We made tacos and wrapped them in foil to eat later during a break from the field work. We quickly put on our working clothes, which consist of a pair of old blue jeans, old tennis shoes, a cotton T-shirt, a long-sleeve shirt to go over it, and a hat.

The next, and probably most difficult task, was waking up the children. Calling out their names to arouse them did no good. Neither did shaking them a bit. We found that the only thing that worked was dragging 10-year-old Jimmy from under the covers and into the bathroom to wash his face and get him dressed. With Billy, 7, we had a harder time. Maria Elena had to kneel beside him and dress him while he was still sound asleep on the floor.

By this time it was usually 4:45 a.m., and we had to be in the fields at 5 o'clock. So we quickly piled into the car and took our 10-minute drive into Milton-Freewater to the raspberry field. During the short drive, the cool morning breeze and the music blaring from the radio woke everyone up and the children started talking about how they would spend the money they hoped to earn that day. One of the things that impressed me most about the Martinez family is how at an early age the children learn the importance of work. They know that without working, there is no money.

Once we arrived in the fields, everyone immediately went to work, since they knew what to do—except me. I had to keep asking them questions, observing what they did while I followed in their footsteps. Picking raspberries is not hard physical labor, but it is tedious. The children and Maria Elena moved through the raspberry fields, fighting their way through weeded rows. With their hands and arms they moved the slightly thorned vines out of the way to get to the raspberries. Within just a few minutes, I found that my arms and hands were scratched from the thorns. The children laughed at me because I was constantly yelling, "Ouch!" Our hands were also covered with the red juice of the berries.

After about an hour, the children started getting tired, especially Billy. So instead of picking berries, we put him to work as an errand boy getting us water and more empty flats. Later, the boys decided that all they wanted to do was play. In two instances, the boys were running up and down the rows and stumbled on one of the flats we had filled, spilling all of the raspberries onto the ground. I couldn't help but laugh. Maria Elena became furious, and I later learned why.

In the five hours we worked, we filled 14 flats. Two days later when we went to pick up our pay we found we earned $23. At that moment, I remembered the two flats the boys stumbled over. I realized how precious every picked raspberry is in order to earn money to support a family. The children thought $23 was a sufficient amount. Maria Elena didn't say anything.

I thought, "How can farm workers survive like this? They work such long hours to barely earn a penny?" Putting it in terms I'm familiar with, I divided the amount earned into the hours worked to find that it came to about $4.60 an hour. However, there were four of us working, so it really added up to only $1.15 an hour. This is how some migrant families live year after year.

After thinking about it for a while, Maria Elena has decided she no longer wants to pick berries. "It's not worth the time for the small amount that is earned," she exclaims.

The children, however, keep insisting that once

their father finished his temporary jobs and joined us in the fields, the money earned would increase. Charlie, too, said he wanted to continue working in the fields on the days he was not scheduled to work at his temporary job at the YWCA.

"Even if we make only $5, that's better than sitting at home not earning anything," he tells his mother. I learned that Charlie, at age 15, already has the worker's mentality of his father—it's a necessity to do any type of work because money is needed. Charlie goes to sleep repeatedly asking his mother, "Are we going to go pick berries in the morning?" The younger children go to sleep begging their mother not to take them to the field in the morning.

With everyone asleep on the floor, on mattresses or on the sofa in our four-room rental home, I lay awake on my mattress thinking about the flats that were stumbled over. . . .

Fall Harvest: No Jobs

Through the summer, unusual weather plagues the Walla Walla area and other parts of the country, causing severe damage. Crops freeze or are washed away. Farmers throughout Walla Walla note that June's heavy rains are causing portions of the sweet onion crop to rot, some reporting that up to 25 percent of the crop is damaged. So, fewer farm workers are needed. In some cases, farmers hire crews, but then don't have enough work for them. The word circulating among the migrant community is that work in the fields is hard to find not only in Walla Walla but anywhere in the country.

"Some of the migrant families that we met in Pasco went up to the Seattle coast when the asparagus finished last month and now they are heading back to Texas because they couldn't find any work," Maria Elena says. These families were expecting to pick blueberries and raspberries, but found coastal crops damaged by cold weather.

"It costs more money traveling looking for work than it would returning to Texas. You spend money on gas and food, and if you're going to spend the night somewhere then you try to cram everyone into a $20 a night hotel. After all this, you hopefully try to save a little of the money you earned working in the fields. That's why sometimes it's better to go home with the little money you make than try to travel around looking for more work."

Maria Elena says it costs about $300 in gas, plus food and lodging, to get from Washington to Texas. "Right now that is my biggest worry, that we won't have enough money for the road, much less for the winter when we don't work."

The murmur among the migrant families is that work can still be found in Minnesota and as far away as Florida, but will families take the risk of traveling that far and finding a situation similar to the one here?

"I don't know," Maria Elena says, sounding wary. "I have no idea what my husband has planned." As it turned out, the Martinezes didn't have to go that far.

The Search for Work: To Boardman, Oregon

After three unsuccessful weeks of looking for steady work in the Walla Walla area, Raul and Maria Elena and their three boys have packed all their belongings into their truck and moved about 90 miles southwest to Boardman, Oregon. Raul could not support his family on the few temporary jobs he was getting in Walla Walla, and the fact that some days found him without work left him feeling desperate.

"We don't like to have little jobs here and there, we like to have something where we know we will be working for at least a few weeks to a month," Raul says in Spanish.

"For example, before we went to Walla Walla we were in Pasco, picking asparagus, and that was from April to June and we liked that," Maria Elena explains. "But working every now and then and then having some days when we don't have work at all is something we're not used to."

Last year, the Martinezes worked the potato harvest in Boardman, and that is what they hope to do this year. So far, Raul has earned about $300 working at odd jobs while in Walla Walla and about $4,000 cutting asparagus in Pasco. Charlie was earning about $100 a week in his summer job at the YWCA, and he still had about a month left of work. The money he was earning would have helped him buy his school clothes this fall, but his father still felt that it was best for the family to leave Walla Walla and look for work elsewhere.

"My husband is the one that supports the family and even though Charlie was earning good money at a fun job, we had to leave so Raul could find a job," Maria Elena says. "Besides, Charlie can find a job working anywhere with his father."

Raul and Maria Elena's eldest son, Raul Martinez Jr., 34, his wife Iris, and their 4-year-old daughter Abby, are also in Boardman where Raul Jr. is working at Columbia Livestock, a local farm owned by Bob Muller. Like his father, Raul Jr. migrates from LaGrulla to the northwest part of the country every year in search of work. Raul Sr. hopes to get a job working with his son: "I worked [at that farm] last year and they know me and they know that I am a hard worker so I think I will be hired again this year."

"We hope he gets a job here or else we have to see where else we go," Maria Elena says.

With the move, the family has to resettle in a new rental apartment, in a new community, in a new state.

But even if the location is new, there are many circumstances that remain the same. There is the task of having to pack and unpack a truck, stock up on food, go to the local welfare department to sign up for food stamps, and visit the food bank to see what food they can get.

The task of looking for housing was not difficult. The family immediately found a vacancy in an apartment complex where they had stayed before. The welfare department will defray the $275 (plus utilities) monthly rent, and the Martinezes are not required to put down a deposit. The apartment is unfurnished, so Raul and Maria Elena contact friends of relatives to see if anyone has some furniture that can be spared.

As Maria Elena spends the evening of their first day in their new home unpacking and putting things away in kitchen cupboards, she gives a deep sigh and repeats a common theme, "How horrible it is to always have to keep moving. It really tires you out, but that's the only way we can live."

Three Rules for Life on the Road

Never make plans. Always be ready to move. Adjust.

If there is anything I am learning about migrant living, it is the three rules above. It amazes me how families can decide overnight to move out of their current residence and into a new community, and how they immediately pack all their belongings, load their trucks, and are ready to hit the road early the next morning.

When the Martinez family moved from Pasco to Walla Walla on July 1, what struck me the most was that within four hours, they had cleared out of their trailer in Pasco, moved to Walla Walla, unpacked, and "set up house" in a rental apartment in the south side of the city. Now, at the end of July, they did the exact same thing during their move to Boardman. It took me one full night and an entire morning just to pack my bedroom.

Another important aspect I've learned from the Martinezes is "don't establish ties with anyone or anything." I learned we were moving to Boardman one day in advance. This meant having to pack immediately. Aside from that, I still had an apartment lease to attend to, utilities to take care of, banking to do, forwarding addresses to leave, plans to cancel, and farewells to say.

The Martinezes packed and left.

This is how they are used to living. They purposely try to find housing in labor camps where rent is paid on a weekly or monthly basis. Rule No. 1: long-range plans are not made.

When they are setting up house, they unpack only the necessities. Clothes usually remain stored in large green trash bags, and are unpacked as needed. Rule No. 2: always be ready to move.

What I also find amazing is how they quickly find comfort in strange and unfamiliar surroundings. The Martinezes had no trouble in setting up house in Walla Walla or now in Boardman. Upon arrival, the two younger boys, Billy and Jimmy, roamed the neighborhood in search of new friends or old ones. Charlie, like his father, will walk about the apartment inspecting things and checking out what needs to be fixed, if anything. And Maria Elena will head to the kitchen to familiarize herself with the stove, oven, and other appliances.

Their first night is passed with sound, restful sleep. I'm usually tossing and turning. This is where Rule No. 3 comes in: adjust.

With the amount of time migrant families spend on the road, it's no wonder that they live by these three rules. However, when they have settled in to field work for awhile, other guidelines are observed.

"It's Good to Be a Hard Worker"

When members of the Martinez family speak of "el patron," or the boss, they usually speak highly of him. Raul, who has been working in the fields since he was a young boy, says that a good "patron" is someone who will let his employees bring home some of the food that has been harvested.

"Some of the 'patrones' will leave boxes and boxes of the fruit or vegetable out in the fields so that the poor people can come and get what they need for free," he says. "Those are the ones we like because it shows us that they are willing to give what they have to others who don't have much."

In each field that Raul has been working, he has been able to gather some of the crop and bring it home with him each evening. In the past few months, the apartment has been filled with burlap sacks of potatoes, tomatoes, onions, and now apples. And since there is such an abundance of vegetables and fruits, the Martinezes share what they have with relatives and neighbors.

Another important aspect of a good boss is his understanding in cases where workers are ill. The Martinezes have not had any problems in this regard either.

"Well, Raul won't go to the doctor if he gets sick, but that's because he doesn't want to miss one day's work. It has nothing to do with the boss," says Maria Elena. "But in the times that I've gotten sick and not showed up to work, the boss will always tell my husband, 'That's a good reason.'"

The Martinezes say they have always had a good rapport with their employers and have never complained of lack of water or other facilities. And every year they are called back to work with the same farmers.

"These people know I am a good, hard worker and they all want me back. I don't believe in being lazy," says Raul. "There are some people who will try to goof off when they work, but that doesn't get them anywhere because all that happens is they end up getting fired."

When working in the fields, Raul is usually the first one out hoeing or picking. He never misses a day. He usually stays until the sun is about to set, and sometimes he is known to skip his lunch break because he doesn't want to miss a minute's work. He attributes the fact that he has proven himself as the reason he is always called back or referred from one farmer to another.

He believes that people must work hard in order to be treated right, and that is something he has instilled in his children. When Charlie was working the fields with him, Charlie could sometimes be heard complaining about the job. His father would always turn around and say in Spanish, "Be quiet, Charlie, and start working. Don't be lazy! It's good to be a hard worker. And if 'el patron' sees that you do good work, then they will always call you back." Raul's work ethic has given him an advantage over hundreds of migrant workers who compete seasonally for jobs.

Those Left in Line

Prior to the start of harvest, migrant workers—both men and women, young and old—rush to the personnel office to submit applications for employment. This year, word spreads quickly throughout the migrant community that workers are needed to harvest potatoes, onions, apples, and other crops. As early as 6 a.m., lines begin to form as people crowd around the locked entrance doors. Those waiting in line are full of questions. "I wonder how many workers they'll need this year?" "I wonder how long the harvest will last?" "I wonder how much they pay?" "I wonder if I'll get hired?"

A few hours later, movement can be seen indoors and excitement builds outside. But by this time the number of people waiting to apply has grown from about 20 to a couple of hundred. The doors open and people enter shoving and pushing, racing to sign their names on a sheet of paper with the rest of the applicants. They know that the lower their names appear on the list, the less chance they have for getting hired.

For the past few weeks, I've placed myself among the migrant workers seeking employment. I go with Maria Elena and some of her friends and relatives, and am careful not to say a word. Maria Elena speaks for all of us, and when I do talk, it's only in Spanish. In some cases, I've had to fill out applications that ask for past field work experience. I fill in the blanks with the word "none." Maria Elena says I have to come up with a believable explanation as to why I haven't worked before. We create the following scenario: I was married, but my husband left me and I now have to support myself and my three children. I never had to use that explanation, however, because I was never hired.

This application process taught me two things: migrant workers are most likely to be rehired by employers for whom they worked before, or where they are recommended by someone whose opinion is respected. Luckily, the Martinez family has had little difficulty in finding work. They have excellent recommendations and are always called back.

"We're hard workers, and everyone knows that. They know we like to work and that I don't believe in being lazy," Raul says in Spanish.

Three weeks ago, Raul and Maria Elena were called to work to pick apples for Western Empires Corporation, located about seven miles east of Boardman. They were recommended for the job by the landlord of their apartment complex. Maria Elena was unable to go because of medical problems, but Raul has gone to the fields every day from 7 a.m. to about 5 p.m. Raul has never picked apples before, but says he likes it. However, every night his wife rubs his shoulders and back to help ease the pain. He has fallen off the ladder three times in the orchard.

"Pay is good," Raul says. "We get $7 for each box we fill." He normally fills eight boxes a day, but sometimes it's 10 and other days only six. The money will be used to get the family back to Texas this fall.

Every afternoon, Raul will come home with sacks filled with apples he has picked. "The patron is real nice. He lets us bring home some of the fruit," Raul says. Lately, the apartment has been filled with the aroma of freshly baked apple pies. The family shares what it has with other family members and friends. Although the Martinez family hasn't suffered from lack of work, hundreds of others have. When I was notified that I would not be hired, I shrugged it off.

"I really don't need this job," I thought. "I'm just doing it to see what it's like." But I looked around me and saw many others who also were not hired. Their faces were filled with despair. Men and women carrying babies in their arms walked slowly to their cars after they were told there would be no room for them in the harvest. Words aren't spoken but their eyes ask, "Now what?" As one couple was getting into their car, the woman told her husband, "Don't worry. You still have applications in at two other farms. One of those will hire you."

Near one car, a group of about five men were

huddled around, each one of them shaking his head and complaining in Spanish, "If they know they are only going to need 65 people in their crew, then why do they sign up over 200 people? All that is doing is giving the rest of us false hope." Another man said, "They should say right from the beginning that they are going to hire those that worked last year."

Shortly, another man approaches and tells them that applications are going to be taken the next day to work the potato harvest. With a deep sigh, one man says, "Well then, we'll go tomorrow and see what they tell us there."

Latin Women Pray

by Judith Ortiz Cofer

*In the stories "A Prayer" and ". . . And the
Earth Did Not Devour Him," Chicana
women pray heartbreakingly for the health
of their loved ones, but it seems that God
does not listen. This poem by a Puerto
Rican writer also depicts Latina women in
prayer. Notice the image of God offered to
these women. How does this image reflect
the society they find themselves in?*

Latin women pray
In incense sweet churches
They pray in Spanish to an Anglo God
With a Jewish heritage.
5   And this Great White Father
Imperturbable in his marble pedestal
Looks down upon his brown daughters
Votive candles shining like lust
In his all seeing eyes
10   Unmoved by their persistent prayers.

Yet year after year
Before his image they kneel
Margarita Josefina Maria and Isabel
All fervently hoping
15   That if not omnipotent
At least he be bilingual

Napa, California

by Ana Castillo

*This poem, like Rivera's novel, describes
how it feels to be a migrant farm worker.
The poem is dedicated to César Chávez, a
Chicano labor leader who led a five-year
strike against California grape growers in
the 1960s. What do the workers lose in
the grape fields? What compels them to
follow their leader?*

We pick
   the bittersweet grapes
   at harvest
   one
5   by
       one
with leather worn hands
        as they pick
        at our dignity
10   and wipe our pride
       away
       like the sweat we wipe
       from our sun-beaten brows
       at midday
15 In fields
   so vast
   that our youth seems
   to pass before us
   and we have grown
20   very
     very
       old
        by dusk . . .

> *(bueno pues, ¿qué vamos a hacer,*
>   *Ambrosio?*
25   *¡bueno pues, seguirle, compadre,*
>   *seguirle!*
> *¡Ay, Mamá!*
> *Sí pues, ¿qué vamos a hacer,*
>   *compadre?*
> *¡Seguirle, Ambrosio, seguirle!)* *

We pick
30   with a desire
   that only survival
   inspires
While the end
   of each day only brings
35   a tired night
   that waits for the sun
   and the land
   that in turn waits
   for us . . .

---

* Well then, what are we going to do, Ambrosio?
  Well then, follow him, my good friend, follow him!
  Mama!
  Yes, well, what are we going to do, friend?
  Follow him, Ambrosio, follow him!

The Plan of Delano

by the National Farm Workers Association

Rivera's novel documents the suffering of Mexican-American migrant workers; at the same time it presents migrants as a community worthy of respect. Compare Rivera's fictional community to the portrayal of the migrant community in "The Plan of Delano," one of the earliest proclamations of César Chávez's National Farm Workers Association. This proclamation was issued in the spring of 1966, as union members marched 250 miles from Delano, California, where their grape strike had begun, to the state capital of Sacramento.

We, the undersigned, gathered in Pilgrimage to the capital of the State in Sacramento in penance for all the failings of Farm Workers as free and sovereign men, do solemnly declare before the civilized world which judges our actions, and before the nation to which we belong, the propositions we have formulated to end the injustice that oppresses us.

We are conscious of the historical significance of our Pilgrimage. It is clearly evident that our path travels through a valley well known to all Mexican farm workers. We know all of these towns of Delano, Madera, Fresno, Modesto, Stockton and Sacramento, because along this very same road, in this very same valley, the Mexican race has sacrificed itself for the last hundred years. Our sweat and our blood have fallen on this land to make other men rich. This Pilgrimage is a witness to the suffering we have seen for generations.

The Penance we accept symbolizes the suffering we shall have in order to bring justice to these same towns, to this same valley. The Pilgrimage we make symbolizes the long historical road we have travelled in this valley alone, and the long road we have yet to travel, with much penance, in order to bring about the Revolution we need, and for which we present the propositions in the following PLAN:

1. This is the beginning of a social movement in fact and not in pronouncements. We seek our basic, God-given rights as human beings. Because we have suffered—and are not afraid to suffer—in order to survive, we are ready to give up everything, even our lives, in our fight for social justice. We shall do it without violence because that is our destiny. To the ranchers, and to all those who oppose us, we say, in the words of Benito Juarez, "EL RESPETO AL DERECHO AJENO ES LA PAZ." [Respect for the rights of others is peace.]

2. We seek the support of all political groups and protection of the government, which is also our government, in our struggle. For too many years we have been treated like the lowest of the low. Our wages and working conditions have been determined from above, because irresponsible legislators who could have helped us, have supported the rancher's argument that the plight of the Farm Worker was a "special case." They saw the obvious effects of an unjust system, starvation wages, contractors, day hauls, forced migration, sickness, illiteracy, camps and sub-human living conditions, and acted as if they were irremediable causes. The farm worker has been

abandoned to his own fate—without representation, without power—subject to mercy and caprice of the rancher. We are tired of words, of betrayals, of indifference. To the politicians we say that the years are gone when the farm worker said nothing and did nothing to help himself. From this movement shall spring leaders who shall understand us, lead us, be faithful to us, and we shall elect them to represent us. we shall be heard.

3. We seek, and have, the support of the Church in what we do. At the head of the Pilgrimage we carry LA VIRGEN DE LA GUADALUPE because she is ours, all ours, Patroness of the Mexican people. We also carry the Sacred Cross and the Star of David because we are not sectarians, and because we ask the help and prayers of all religions. All men are brothers, sons of the same God; that is why we say to all men of good will, in the words of Pope Leo XII, "Everyone's first duty is to protect the workers from the greed of speculators who use human beings as instruments to provide themselves with money. It is neither just nor human to oppress men with excessive work to the point where their minds become enfeebled and their bodies worn out." GOD SHALL NOT ABANDON US.

4. We are suffering. We have suffered, and we are not afraid to suffer in order to win our cause. We have suffered unnumbered ills and crimes in the name of the Law of the Land. Our men, women, and children have suffered not only the basic brutality of stoop labor, and the most obvious injustices of the system; they have also suffered the desperation of knowing that that system caters to the greed of callous men and not to our needs. Now we will suffer for the purpose of ending the poverty, the misery, and the injustice, with the hope that our children will not be exploited as we have been. They have imposed hungers on us,

and now we hunger for justice. We draw our strength from the very despair in which we have been forced to live. WE SHALL ENDURE.

5. We shall unite. We have learned the meaning of UNITY. We know why these United States are just that—united. The strength of the poor is also in union. We know that the poverty of the Mexican or Filipino worker in California is the same as that of all farm workers across the country, the Negroes and poor whites, the Puerto Ricans, Japanese, and Arabians; in short, all of the races that comprise the oppressed minorities of the United States. The majority of the people on our Pilgrimage are of Mexican descent, but the triumph of our race depends on a national association of all farm workers. The ranchers want to keep us divided in order to keep us weak. Many of us have signed individual "work contracts" with the ranchers or contractors, contracts in which they had all the power. These contracts were farces, one more cynical joke at our impotence. That is why we must get together and bargain collectively. We must use the only strength we have, the force of our numbers. The ranchers are few; we are many. UNITED WE SHALL STAND.

6. We shall Strike. We shall pursue the REVOLUTION we have proposed. We are sons of the Mexican Revolution, a revolution of the poor seeking bread and justice. Our revolution will not be armed, but we want the existing social order to dissolve; we want a new social order. We are poor, we are humble, and our only choice is to Strike in those ranches where we are not treated with the respect we deserve as working men, where our rights as free and sovereign men are not recognized. We do not want the paternalism of the rancher; we do not want the contractor; we do not want charity at the price of our dignity. We want to be

equal with all the working men in the nation; we want a just wage, better working conditions, a decent future for our children. To those who oppose us, be they ranchers, police, politicians, or speculators, we say that we are going to continue fighting until we die, or we win. WE SHALL OVERCOME.

Across the San Joaquin Valley, across California, across the entire Southwest of the United States, wherever there are Mexican people, wherever there are farm workers, our movement is spreading like flames across a dry plain. Our PILGRIMAGE is the MATCH that will light our cause for all farm workers to see what is happening here, so that they may do as we have done. The time has come for the liberation of the poor farm worker.

History is on our side.

MAY THE STRIKE GO ON! VIVA LA CAUSA!

The Whistle

by Eudora Welty

*The migrant workers in Rivera's novel are
completely at the mercy of nature and
selfish landowners. Yet they are not the
only workers so vulnerable. See what the
Southern tenant farmers in this story must
sacrifice for their crop.*

Night fell. The darkness was thin, like some sleazy
dress that has been worn and worn for many winters
and always lets the cold through to the bones. Then
the moon rose. A farm lay quite visible, like a white
stone in water, among the stretches of deep woods in
their colorless dead leaf. By a closer and more searching eye than the moon's, everything belonging to the
Mortons might have been seen—even to the tiny
tomato plants in their neat rows closest to the house,
gray and featherlike, appalling in their exposed
fragility. The moonlight covered everything, and lay
upon the darkest shape of all, the farmhouse where
the lamp had just been blown out.

Inside, Jason and Sara Morton were lying between
the quilts of a pallet which had been made up close to
the fireplace. A fire still fluttered in the grate, making
a drowsy sound now and then, and its exhausted light
beat up and down the wall, across the rafters, and
over the dark pallet where the old people lay, like a
bird trying to find its way out of the room.

The long-spaced, tired breathing of Jason was the
only noise besides the flutter of the fire. He lay under
the quilt in a long shape like a bean, turned on his side
to face the door. His lips opened in the dark, and in

and out he breathed, in and out, slowly and with a rise and fall, over and over, like a conversation or a tale— a question and a sigh.

Sara lay on her back with her mouth agape, silent, but not asleep. She was staring at the dark and indistinguishable places among the rafters. Her eyes seemed opened too wide, the lids strained and limp, like openings which have been stretched shapeless and made of no more use. Once a hissing yellow flame stood erect in the old log, and her small face and pale hair, and one hand holding to the edge of the cover, were illuminated for a moment, with shadows bright blue. Then she pulled the quilt clear over her head.

Every night they lay trembling with cold, but no more communicative in their misery than a pair of window shutters beaten by a storm. Sometimes many days, weeks went by without words. They were not really old—they were only fifty; still, their lives were filled with tiredness, with a great lack of necessity to speak, with poverty which may have bound them like a disaster too great for any discussion but left them still separate and undesirous of sympathy. Perhaps, years ago, the long habit of silence may have been started in anger or passion. Who could tell now?

As the fire grew lower and lower, Jason's breathing grew heavy and solemn, and he was even beyond dreams. Completely hidden, Sara's body was as weightless as a strip of cane, there was hardly a shape to the quilt under which she was lying. Sometimes it seemed to Sara herself that it was her lack of weight which kept her from ever getting warm.

She was so tired of the cold! That was all it could do any more—make her tired. Year after year, she felt sure that she would die before the cold was over. Now, according to the Almanac, it was spring. . . . But year after year it was always the same. The plants would be set out in their frames, transplanted always too soon, and there was a freeze. . . . When was the last time they had grown tall and full, that the cold had held off and there was a crop?

Like a vain dream, Sara began to have thoughts of the spring and summer. At first she thought only simply, of the colors of green and red, the smell of the sun on the ground, the touch of leaves and of warm ripening tomatoes. Then, all hidden as she was under the quilt, she began to imagine and remember the town of Dexter in the shipping season. There in her mind, dusty little Dexter became a theater for almost legendary festivity, a place of pleasure. On every road leading in, smiling farmers were bringing in wagon-loads of the most beautiful tomatoes. The packing sheds at Dexter Station were all decorated—no, it was simply that the May sun was shining. Mr. Perkins, the tall, gesturing figure, stood in the very center of everything, buying, directing, waving yellow papers that must be telegrams, shouting with grand impatience. And it was he, after all, that owned their farm now. Train after train of empty freight cars stretched away, waiting and then being filled. Was it possible to have saved out of the threat of the cold so many tomatoes in the world? Of course, for here marched in a perfect parade of Florida packers, all the way from Florida, tanned, stockingless, some of them tattooed. The music box was playing in the café across the way, and the crippled man that walked like a duck was back taking poses for a dime of the young people with their heads together. With shouts of triumph the men were getting drunk, and now and then a pistol went off somewhere. In the shade the children celebrated in tomato fights. A strong, heady, sweet smell hung over everything. Such excitement! Let the packers rest, if only for a moment, thought Sara.

Stretch them out, stained with sweat, under the shade tree, and one can play the guitar. The girl wrappers listen while they work. What small brown hands, red with juice! Their faces are forever sleepy and flushed; when the men speak to them they laugh. . . . And Jason and Sara themselves are standing there, standing under the burning sun near the first shed, giving over their own load, watching their own tomatoes shoved into the process, swallowed away—sorted, wrapped, loaded, dispatched in a freight car —all so fast. . . . Mr. Perkins holds out his hard, quick hand. Shake it fast! How quickly it is all over!

Sara, weightless under the quilt, could think of the celebrations of Dexter and see the vision of ripe tomatoes only in brief snatches, like the flare-up of the little fire. The rest of the time she thought only of cold, of cold going on before and after. She could not help but feel the chill of the here and now, which was not to think at all, but was for her only a trembling in the dark.

She coughed patiently and turned her head to one side. She peered over the quilt just a little and saw that the fire had at last gone out. There was left only a hulk of red log, a still, red, bent shape, like one of Jason's socks thrown down to be darned somehow. With only this to comfort her, Sara closed her eyes and fell asleep.

The husband and wife now lay perfectly still in the dark room, with Jason's hoarse, slow breathing, like the commotion of some clumsy nodding old bear trying to climb a tree, heard by nobody at all.

Every hour it was getting colder and colder. The moon, intense and white as the snow that does not fall here, drew higher in the sky, in the long night, and more distant from the earth. The farm looked as tiny and still as a seashell, with the little knob of a house surrounded by its curved furrows of tomato plants. Cold like a white pressing hand reached down and lay still over the shell.

In Dexter there is a great whistle which is blown when a freeze threatens. It is known everywhere as Mr. Perkins' whistle. Now it sounded out in the clear night, blast after blast. Over the countryside lights appeared in the windows of the farms. Men and women ran out into the fields and covered up their plants with whatever they had, while Mr. Perkins' whistle blew and blew.

Jason Morton was not waked up by the great whistle. On he slept, his cavernous breathing like roars coming from a hollow tree. His right hand had been thrown out, from some deepness he must have dreamed, and lay stretched on the cold floor in the very center of a patch of moonlight which had moved across the room.

Sara felt herself waking. She knew that Mr. Perkins' whistle was blowing, what it meant—and that it now remained for her to get Jason and go out to the field. A soft laxity, an illusion of warmth, flowed stubbornly down her body, and for a few moments she continued to lie still.

Then she was sitting up and seizing her husband by the shoulders, without saying a word, rocking him back and forth. It took all her strength to wake him. He coughed, his roaring was over, and he sat up. He said nothing either, and they both sat with bent heads and listened for the whistle. After a silence it blew again, a long, rising blast.

Promptly Sara and Jason got out of bed. They were both fully dressed, because of the cold, and only needed to put on their shoes. Jason lighted the lantern, and Sara gathered the bedclothes over her arm and followed him out.

Everything was white, and everything looked vast

and extensive to them as they walked over the frozen field. White in a shadowed pit, abandoned from summer to summer, the old sorghum mill stood like the machine of a dream, with its long prostrate pole, its blunted axis.

Stooping over the little plants, Jason and Sara touched them and touched the earth. For their own knowledge, by their hands, they found everything to be true—the cold, the rightness of the warning, the need to act. Over the sticks set in among the plants they laid the quilts one by one, spreading them with a slow ingenuity. Jason took off his coat and laid it over the small tender plants by the side of the house. Then he glanced at Sara, and she reached down and pulled her dress off over her head. Her hair fell down out of its pins, and she began at once to tremble violently. The skirt was luckily long and full, and all the rest of the plants were covered by it.

Then Sara and Jason stood for a moment and stared almost idly at the field and up at the sky.

There was no wind. There was only the intense whiteness of moonlight. Why did this calm cold sink into them like the teeth of a trap? They bent their shoulders and walked silently back into the house.

The room was not much warmer. They had forgotten to shut the door behind them when the whistle was blowing so hard. They sat down to wait for morning.

Then Jason did a rare, strange thing. There long before morning he poured kerosene over some kindling and struck a light to it. Squatting, they got near it, quite gradually they drew together, and sat motionless until it all burned down. Still Sara did not move. Then Jason, in his underwear and long blue trousers, went out and brought in another load, and the big cherry log which of course was meant to be saved for the very last of winter.

The extravagant warmth of the room had sent some

kind of agitation over Sara, like her memories of Dexter in the shipping season. She sat huddled in a long brown cotton petticoat, holding on to the string which went around the waist. Her mouse-colored hair, paler at the temples, was hanging loose down to her shoulders, like a child's unbound for a party. She held her knees against her numb, pendulant breasts and stared into the fire, her eyes widening.

On his side of the hearth Jason watched the fire burn too. His breath came gently, quickly, noiselessly, as though for a little time he would conceal or defend his tiredness. He lifted his arms and held out his misshapen hands to the fire.

At last every bit of the wood was gone. Now the cherry log was burned to ashes.

And all of a sudden Jason was on his feet again. Of all things, he was bringing the split-bottomed chair over to the hearth. He knocked it to pieces. . . . It burned well and brightly. Sara never said a word. She did not move. . . .

Then the kitchen table. To think that a solid, steady four-legged table like that, that had stood thirty years in one place, should be consumed in such a little while! Sara stared almost greedily at the waving flames.

Then when that was over, Jason and Sara sat in darkness where their bed had been, and it was colder than ever. The fire the kitchen table had made seemed wonderful to them—as if what they had never said, and what could not be, had its life, too, after all.

But Sara trembled, again pressing her hard knees against her breast. In the return of winter, of the night's cold, something strange, like fright, or dependency, a sensation of complete helplessness, took possession of her. All at once, without turning her head, she spoke.

"Jason . . ."

A silence. But only for a moment.

"Listen," said her husband's uncertain voice.

They held very still, as before, with bent heads.

Outside, as though it would exact something further from their lives, the whistle continued to blow.

First Confession

by Frank O'Connor

In Rivera's novel, the young narrator of the episode "First Communion" is afraid that he won't remember all the sins he has committed and will, consequently, burn in hell. The narrator of this humorous story, a boy in Ireland, has exactly the same fears. And his confession, like the other boy's, turns out to be quite different from what he expects. Find out what he learns.

All the trouble began when my grandfather died and my grandmother—my father's mother—came to live with us. Relations in the one house are a strain at the best of times, but, to make matters worse, my grandmother was a real old country woman and quite unsuited to the life in town. She had a fat, wrinkled old face, and, to Mother's great indignation, went round the house in bare feet—the boots had her crippled, she said. For dinner she had a jug of porter and a pot of potatoes with—sometimes—a bit of salt fish, and she poured out the potatoes on the table and ate them slowly, with great relish, using her fingers by way of a fork.

Now, girls are supposed to be fastidious, but I was the one who suffered most from this. Nora, my sister, just sucked up to the old woman for the penny she got every Friday out of the old-age pension, a thing I could not do. I was too honest, that was my trouble; and when I was playing with Bill Connell, the sergeant-major's son, and saw my grandmother steering up the path with the jug of porter sticking out from beneath her shawl I was mortified. I made excuses not to let him come into the house, because I could never be sure what she would be up to when we went in.

When Mother was at work and my grandmother made the dinner I wouldn't touch it. Nora once tried to make me, but I hid under the table from her and took the bread-knife with me for protection. Nora let on to be very indignant (she wasn't, of course, but she knew Mother saw through her, so she sided with Gran) and came after me. I lashed out at her with the bread-knife, and after that she left me alone. I stayed there till Mother came in from work and made my dinner, but when Father came in later Nora said in a shocked voice: "Oh, Dadda, do you know what Jackie did at dinnertime?" Then, of course, it all came out; Father gave me a flaking; Mother interfered, and for days after that he didn't speak to me and Mother barely spoke to Nora. And all because of that old woman! God knows, I was heart-scalded.

Then, to crown my misfortunes, I had to make my first Confession and Communion. It was an old woman called Ryan who prepared us for these. She was about the one age with Gran; she was well-to-do, lived in a big house on Montenotte, wore a black cloak and bonnet, and came every day to school at three o'clock when we should have been going home, and talked to us of Hell. She may have mentioned the other place as well, but that could only have been by accident, for Hell had the first place in her heart.

She lit a candle, took out a new half-crown, and offered it to the first boy who would hold one finger—only one finger!—in the flame for five minutes by the school clock. Being always very ambitious I was tempted to volunteer, but I thought it might look greedy. Then she asked were we afraid of holding one finger—only one finger!—in a little candle flame for five minutes and not afraid of burning all over in roasting hot furnaces for all eternity. "All eternity! Just think of that! A whole lifetime goes by and it's nothing, not even a drop in the ocean of your sufferings." The woman was really interesting about Hell, but my attention was all fixed on the half-crown. At the end of the lesson she put it back in her purse. It was a great disappointment; a religious woman like that, you wouldn't think she'd bother about a thing like a half-crown.

Another day she said she knew a priest who woke one night to find a fellow he didn't recognize leaning over the end of his bed. The priest was a bit frightened —naturally enough—but he asked the fellow what he wanted, and the fellow said in a deep, husky voice that he wanted to go to Confession. The priest said it was an awkward time and wouldn't it do in the morning, but the fellow said that last time he went to Confession, there was one sin he kept back, being ashamed to mention it, and now it was always on his mind. Then the priest knew it was a bad case, because the fellow was after making a bad confession and committing a mortal sin. He got up to dress, and just then the cock crew in the yard outside, and—lo and behold!—when the priest looked round there was no sign of the fellow, only a smell of burning timber, and when the priest looked at his bed didn't he see the print of two hands burned in it? That was because the fellow had made a bad confession. This story made a shocking impression on me.

But the worst of all was when she showed us how to examine our conscience. Did we take the name of the Lord, our God, in vain? Did we honor our father and our mother? (I asked her did this include grandmothers and she said it did.) Did we love our neighbor as ourselves? Did we covet our neighbor's goods? (I thought of the way I felt about the penny that Nora got every Friday.) I decided that, between one thing and another, I must have broken the whole ten commandments, all on account of that old woman, and so far as I could see, so long as she remained in the house I had no hope of ever doing anything else.

I was scared to death of Confession. The day the whole class went I let on to have a toothache, hoping my absence wouldn't be noticed; but at three o'clock, just as I was feeling safe, along comes a chap with a message from Mrs. Ryan that I was to go to Confession myself on Saturday and be at the chapel for Communion with the rest. To make it worse, Mother couldn't come with me and sent Nora instead.

Now, that girl had ways of tormenting me that Mother never knew of. She held my hand as we went down the hill, smiling sadly and saying how sorry she was for me, as if she were bringing me to the hospital for an operation.

"Oh, God help us!" she moaned. "Isn't it a terrible pity you weren't a good boy? Oh, Jackie, my heart bleeds for you! How will you ever think of all your sins? Don't forget you have to tell him about the time you kicked Gran on the shin."

"Lemme go!" I said, trying to drag myself free of her. "I don't want to go to Confession at all."

"But sure, you'll have to go to Confession, Jackie," she replied in the same regretful tone. "Sure, if you didn't, the parish priest would be up to the house, looking for you. 'Tisn't, God knows, that I'm not sorry for you. Do you remember the time you tried to kill me with the bread-knife under the table? And the language you used to me? I don't know what he'll do with you at all, Jackie. He might have to send you up to the Bishop."

I remember thinking bitterly that she didn't know the half of what I had to tell—if I told it. I knew I couldn't tell it, and understood perfectly why the fellow in Mrs. Ryan's story made a bad confession; it seemed to me a great shame that people wouldn't stop criticizing him. I remember that steep hill down to the church, and the sunlit hillsides beyond the valley of the river, which I saw in the gaps between the houses like Adam's last glimpse of Paradise.

Then, when she had manoeuvred me down the long flight of steps to the chapel yard, Nora suddenly changed her tone. She became the raging malicious devil she really was.

"There you are!" she said with a yelp of triumph, hurling me through the church door. "And I hope he'll give you the penitential psalms, you dirty little caffler."

I knew then I was lost, given up to eternal justice. The door with the colored-glass panels swung shut behind me, the sunlight went out and gave place to deep shadow, and the wind whistled outside so that the silence within seemed to crackle like ice under my feet. Nora sat in front of me by the confession box. There were a couple of old women ahead of her, and then a miserable-looking poor devil came and wedged me in at the other side, so that I couldn't escape even if I had the courage. He joined his hands and rolled his eyes in the direction of the roof, muttering aspirations in an anguished tone, and I wondered had he a grandmother too. Only a grandmother could account for a fellow behaving in that heartbroken way, but he was better off than I, for he at least could go and confess his sins; while I would make a bad confession and then die in the night and be continually coming back and burning people's furniture.

Nora's turn came, and I heard the sound of something slamming, and then her voice as if butter wouldn't melt in her mouth, and then another slam, and out she came. God, the hypocrisy of women! Her eyes were lowered, her head was bowed, and her hands were joined very low down on her stomach, and she walked up the aisle to the side altar looking like a saint. You never saw such an exhibition of devotion; and I remembered the devilish malice with which she had tormented me all the way from our door, and wondered were all religious people like that, really. It was my turn now. With the fear of damnation in my soul I went in, and the confessional door closed of itself behind me.

It was pitch-dark and I couldn't see priest or anything else. Then I really began to be frightened. In the darkness it was a matter between God and me, and He had all the odds. He knew what my intentions were before I even started; I had no chance. All I had ever been told about Confession got mixed up in my mind, and I knelt to one wall and said: "Bless me, father, for I have sinned; this is my first confession." I waited for a few minutes, but nothing happened, so I tried it on the other wall. Nothing happened there either. He had me spotted all right.

It must have been then that I noticed the shelf at about one height with my head. It was really a place for grown-up people to rest their elbows, but in my distracted state I thought it was probably the place you were supposed to kneel. Of course, it was on the high side and not very deep, but I was always good at climbing and managed to get up all right. Staying up was the trouble. There was room only for my knees, and nothing you could get a grip on but a sort of wooden molding a bit above it. I held on to the molding and repeated the words a little louder, and this time something happened all right. A slide was slammed back; a little light entered the box, and a man's voice said: "Who's there?"

"'Tis me, father," I said for fear he mightn't see me and go away again. I couldn't see him at all. The place the voice came from was under the molding, about level with my knees, so I took a good grip of the molding and swung myself down till I saw the astonished face of a young priest looking up at me. He had to put his head on one side to see me, and I had to put mine on one side to see him, so we were more or less talking to one another upside-down. It struck me as a queer way of hearing confessions, but I didn't feel it my place to criticize.

"Bless me, father, for I have sinned; this is my first confession," I rattled off all in one breath, and swung myself down the least shade more to make it easier for him.

"What are you doing up there?" he shouted in an angry voice, and the strain the politeness was putting on my hold of the molding, and the shock of being addressed in such an uncivil tone, were too much for me. I lost my grip, tumbled, and hit the door an unmerciful wallop before I found myself flat on my back in the middle of the aisle. The people who had been waiting stood up with their mouths open. The priest opened the door of the middle box and came out, pushing his biretta back from his forehead; he looked something terrible. Then Nora came scampering down the aisle.

"Oh, you dirty little caffler!" she said. "I might have known you'd do it. I might have known you'd disgrace me. I can't leave you out of my sight for one minute."

Before I could even get to my feet to defend myself she bent down and gave me a clip across the ear. This reminded me that I was so stunned I had even forgotten to cry, so that people might think I wasn't hurt at all, when in fact I was probably maimed for life. I gave a roar out of me.

"What's all this about?" the priest hissed, getting angrier than ever and pushing Nora off me. "How dare you hit the child like that, you little vixen?"

"But I can't do my penance with him, father," Nora

cried, cocking an outraged eye up at him.

"Well, go and do it, or I'll give you some more to do," he said, giving me a hand up. "Was it coming to Confession you were, my poor man?" he asked me.

"'Twas, father," said I with a sob.

"Oh," he said respectfully, "a big hefty fellow like you must have terrible sins. Is this your first?"

"'Tis, father," said I.

"Worse and worse," he said gloomily. "The crimes of a lifetime. I don't know will I get rid of you at all today. You'd better wait now till I'm finished with these old ones. You can see by the looks of them they haven't much to tell."

"I will, father," I said with something approaching joy.

The relief of it was really enormous. Nora stuck out her tongue at me from behind his back, but I couldn't even be bothered retorting. I knew from the very moment that man opened his mouth that he was intelligent above the ordinary. When I had time to think, I saw how right I was. It only stood to reason that a fellow confessing after seven years would have more to tell than people that went every week. The crimes of a lifetime, exactly as he said. It was only what he expected, and the rest was the cackle of old women and girls with their talk of Hell, the Bishop, and the penitential psalms. That was all they knew. I started to make my examination of conscience, and barring the one bad business of my grandmother it didn't seem so bad.

The next time, the priest steered me into the confession box himself and left the shutter back the way I could see him get in and sit down at the further side of the grille from me.

"Well, now," he said, "what do they call you?"

"Jackie, father," said I.

"And what's a-trouble to you, Jackie?"

"Father," I said, feeling I might as well get it over while I had him in good humor, "I had it all arranged to kill my grandmother."

He seemed a bit shaken by that, all right, because he said nothing for quite a while.

"My goodness," he said at last, "that'd be a shocking thing to do. What put that into your head?"

"Father," I said, feeling very sorry for myself, "she's an awful woman."

"Is she?" he asked. "What way is she awful?"

"She takes porter, father," I said, knowing well from the way Mother talked of it that this was a mortal sin, and hoping it would make the priest take a more favorable view of my case.

"Oh, my!" he said, and I could see he was impressed.

"And snuff, father," said I.

"That's a bad case, sure enough, Jackie," he said.

"And she goes round in her bare feet, father," I went on in a rush of self-pity, "and she knows I don't like her, and she gives pennies to Nora and none to me, and my da sides with her and flakes me, and one night I was so heart-scalded I made up my mind I'd have to kill her."

"And what would you do with the body?" he asked with great interest.

"I was thinking I could chop that up and carry it away in a barrow I have," I said.

"Begor, Jackie," he said, "do you know you're a terrible child?"

"I know, father," I said, for I was just thinking the same thing myself. "I tried to kill Nora too with a bread-knife under the table, only I missed her."

"Is that the little girl that was beating you just now?" he asked.

"'Tis, father."

"Someone will go for her with a bread-knife one

day, and he won't miss her," he said rather cryptically. "You must have great courage. Between ourselves, there's a lot of people I'd like to do the same to but I'd never have the nerve. Hanging is an awful death."

"Is it, father?" I asked with the deepest interest—I was always very keen on hanging. "Did you ever see a fellow hanged?"

"Dozens of them," he said solemnly. "And they all died roaring."

"Jay!" I said.

"Oh, a horrible death!" he said with great satisfaction. "Lots of the fellows I saw killed their grandmothers too, but they all said 'twas never worth it."

He had me there for a full ten minutes talking, and then walked out the chapel yard with me. I was genuinely sorry to part with him, because he was the most entertaining character I'd ever met in the religious line. Outside, after the shadow of the church, the sunlight was like the roaring of waves on a beach; it dazzled me; and when the frozen silence melted and I heard the screech of trams on the road my heart soared. I knew now I wouldn't die in the night and come back, leaving marks on my mother's furniture. It would be a great worry to her, and the poor soul had enough.

Nora was sitting on the railing, waiting for me, and she put on a very sour puss when she saw the priest with me. She was mad jealous because a priest had never come out of the church with her.

"Well," she asked coldly, after he left me, "what did he give you?"

"Three Hail Marys," I said.

"Three Hail Marys," she repeated incredulously. "You mustn't have told him anything."

"I told him everything," I said confidently.

"About Gran and all?"

"About Gran and all."

(All she wanted was to be able to go home and say I'd made a bad confession.)

"Did you tell him you went for me with the bread-knife?" she asked with a frown.

"I did to be sure."

"And he only gave you three Hail Marys?"

"That's all."

She slowly got down from the railing with a baffled air. Clearly, this was beyond her. As we mounted the steps back to the main road she looked at me suspiciously.

"What are you sucking?" she asked.

"Bullseyes."

"Was it the priest gave them to you?"

"'Twas."

"Lord God," she wailed bitterly, "some people have all the luck! 'Tis no advantage to anybody trying to be good. I might just as well be a sinner like you."

Fourth Grade Ukus (1952)

by Marie Hara

Rivera's story "It's That It Hurts" recounts a migrant boy's painful experience at a Northern school. The following story, by a Hawaiian of Japanese descent, describes children's school experiences before Hawaii became a state in 1959. At the time, most Japanese in Hawaii were descendants of contract workers who had labored on sugar plantations much as Mexicans labored on ranches in Texas and California. Hawaiian society in the 1950s was dominated by white Americans; the Japanese, along with other Asians, Portuguese, and native Hawaiians, held a lower social position. The pidgin English that many nonwhites spoke was viewed as something to be eradicated, like ukus, or lice. Students' fluency in English determined which type of public school they would attend—a prestigious English Standard school (which accepted mostly whites), or a less desirable non–English Standard school.

"Da bolocano," I repeated politely at the cone-shaped mountain where a spiral of smoke signaled into the crayon-shaded air. She must have drawn it.

The woman tester was young and Japanese and smiley. I relaxed, thought for sure I wouldn't have to act "put on" with her. But she kept after me to say the printed words on the picture cards she, unsmiling, held before my eyes.

She shook her head. "Again."

"Da bolocano," I repeated loudly. Maybe, like O-jiji, she couldn't hear. "We wen' go see da bolocano," I explained confidentially to her. And what a big flat puka it was, I thought, ready to tell her the picture made a mistake.

"It's the vol-cano," she enunciated clearly, forcing me to watch her mouth move aggressively. She continued with downcast eyes, "'We went to see the vol-cano.' You can go and wait outside, okay?"

Outside I wondered why—if she had seen it—she drew it all wrong.

Mama shrugged it off as we trudged home.

"Neva mind. Get too many stuck shet ladies ova dere. People no need act, Lei. You wait. You gon' get one good education, not like me."

That was how I ended up at Kaahumanu School, which was non-English Standard, but sported massive flower beds of glowing red and yellow canna lilies arranged in neat rows, which were weeded and watered daily by the students. Teachers at Kaahumanu were large in size, often Hawaiian or Portuguese with only an occasional wiry Chinese or Japanese. There was a surprise haole teacher who came in to teach art and hug kids. Many teachers wore bright hibiscus blooms stuck into their "pugs" of upswept hair. They didn't hold back on any emotions as they swept through the main yard like part of a tide of orderliness, lining up their wriggly classes. They cuffed the bad and patted the heads of the obedient as they counted us. They were magnetic forces with commanding voices, backbones at full attention and bright flowers perched like flags on the tops of their heads. When we stood in formation, the first ritual of the morning, rumors of all kinds went through our lines. I learned that on special holidays the cafeteria might even serve laulaus and poi, which we would help to prepare. Now that was worth waiting for.

I was in a dreamy mood when I first ran into Mrs. Vincente, who was to be my teacher. As a human being she was an impressive creation since her bulk was unsettling and her head quite small. As she waddle-walked toward me, I made a fatal error. I mistook her for an illustration in a library book I had grown fond of in Kohala. She was a dead ringer for the character I thought I was seeing right before my nose. And why not? The first day of school was the beginning of a new chapter in my life. Everything so far had been surprising.

Therefore, I squealed out loud in pleasure, "Oh, Mrs. Piggy-Winkle!" at the sight of the pink-fleshed mountain topped by a salad-plate-sized, orange hibiscus. Did I truly think she would be equally delighted to see me? Mrs. Vincente, as I learned later, would never forget me. At the moment of our meeting, she grabbed me by the back of my neck and shook me fiercely until I blubbered.

Teachers came running; students formed a mob around us, and the school principal, Mrs. Kealoha-Henry, saved me.

As I stood sobbing and shivering from the wild shaking, Mrs. Vincente lectured me on good manners. I shook my head, no-no, when she asked in an emotional voice, "Do you understand?" It took all of Mrs. Kealoha-Henry's counsel to keep Mrs. Vincente away from me.

Grabbing the opportunity, I ran all the way back home where, after she came home from work, Mama found me hiding out in the laundry shed. I didn't return to school for several days after that. But my mother's continual nagging, bribery and just plain boredom finally wore me down. I vowed not to talk at school, in the name of personal safety. And I would forget imagination.

Hanging high on the wall against the painted white wood, positioned to face the person entering up the broad steps through the columned entrance was a large portrait of Queen Kaahumanu, our school's namesake. I studied her fully fleshed face, the insignia of rank in the background and her guarded expression. In return her eyes reviewed me, a small girl who wasn't sure what to do next.

As I stalled and paced the corridor, the morning bell rang and all the other children disappeared. Alone in my patch of indecision, I balanced on one bare foot and then the other while I studied the ancient lady's clear-eyed regard.

When Mrs. Kealoha-Henry found me, she laughed in surprise.

"So you did come back. And now you have met the Queen. Do you know her story? No? I thought so."

The principal, a plump woman who wore old-fashioned glasses, which dangled from a neckpiece onto the front of her shirtwaist, told me then and there about Queen Kaahumanu, the Kuhina Nui. I learned that she was a favorite child and a favorite wife, that her hair was called ehu, meaning that it was reddish unlike that of other Hawaiians of her time, and that she was hapa—of mixed blood, probably from Spanish ancestors. Mrs. Kealoha-Henry suspected the Conquistadors, whose helmets the Hawaiian alii had copied in feathers, had been the first Europeans to Hawaii. I heard the kindly stranger saying that I, too, must be hapa. She suggested a visit to the school library where I would be welcome to read more about the Queen and what she did with the tremendous power she held at the end of her life. Mrs. Kealoha-Henry put her hands on my shoulders and turned me in the direction of the steps that led to the second floor. She would take care of the absences.

Although I hoped that the principal had not confused me with someone else who was Hawaiian by blood, I was very pleased with the thrilling story. Her comments became the bond between the Queen and me. I felt lucky that I went to a school where a hapa was the boss, in fact, commanded tribute. After all, I did have the reddish hair—or some of it—and if I was hapa as she said, then that was the reason for my being different from the others. I felt clearer whenever I looked at Queen Kaahumanu's portrait from then on. Every day the Queen's round face gave me a signal that I was okay; a small thing, but necessary for someone so hungry for signs.

Still, no matter how hard I squinted, the hair depicted in the painting showed no sign of being red. Never mind, I told myself, she was right there, up high, and she looked at me affectionately, if I kept up the squint. Whenever I needed to, I found my way back to the hallway to stand in the breeze and acknowledge the power of our kinship.

"Psssssssst . . ."

I felt a nudge from one side and a soft pinch from the other.

Just before the first morning bell rang, the whispers traveled around. We were aware that our teacher was moving down the line to study each one of us. Our voices were high, and our faces as busy as the noisy birds in the banyan outside. Always chattering, always in tune with our buddies, always watching, we knew how to move together without getting caught. We studied how to do it.

"Joseph. Make quick. We gotta line up; no talk. Standup-straight. Sing loud or she gon' make us guys sing one mo' time."

"She checking the guys' clothes first, if clean or

what. Bum-bye she gon' look our finganail and den check our hair behind the eah, l'dat."

The clanging bell brought us to silent attention.

Joseph looked completely blank. Unconcerned, he, being new, had no understanding of the importance of our morning ritual. He didn't even pretend to mouth the words of Mrs. Vincente's favorite greeting, "Good Morning, Dear Tea-cha, Goooood Mor-ning to You."

Before I could answer importantly, "Cuz got ukus, some guys, you stupid doo-doo head," and think, "But not us guys," our teacher was standing right in front of us. Mrs. Vincente looked grim. Her gold-rimmed eyeglasses gave off glints in the pools of sunlight, evidence of real daylight outside, which invaded our dark, wood-paneled classroom.

She was the one who taught us to sing "Old Plantation Nani Ole" (Oooll . . . Plan-tay-shun . . . Na-ni . . . Ohlay) and "Ma-sa's (never her way, Massa's) in the Cold, Cold Ground," her favorite mournful melodies. She had turned to making us sing in order to drill us on our English skills, so lacking were we in motivation.

Frequently Mrs. Vincente spoke sharply to us about the inappropriate silences of our group. She complained that too often we spoke out of turn but "rarely contributed to the discussion." She must have believed that we didn't absorb anything that she lectured about repeatedly. She often confided aloud that she was "disappointed in" us or we had "disappointed Teacher" or she was "sorry to have to disappoint" us, "however," we had done something wrong again.

She was a puzzle.

The Oriental kids—for that was our label—in the room knew better than to open their mouths just to lose face, and the part-Hawaiian kids knew they would get lickings one way or another if they talked, so we all firmly agreed that silence was golden.

Never would an adult female loom up as large to me as Mrs. Vincente did then. I could see her face only when I sat at a safe distance with a desk for protection. If she approached—in all her girth she was most graceful moving across her neatly waxed floor—her hands took my complete attention. When they were ready to direct us, I felt the way I did when Mama showed me what the red light at the crosswalk was for. When Teacher stood very near me, I couldn't see her tiny eyes, because the soft underpart of her delicate chin transfixed me so that I could not understand the words she mouthed.

Once I overheard her passionate argument with another teacher who wanted to introduce the hula in our P.E. exercises. Mrs. V.'s reasoning escaped me, but I knew she was against it. I stayed hidden in the ti leaves under her window just to hear the rush of her escaping emotions as she grew angrier.

Mrs. Vincente's face was often averted from the horrors she saw represented in the existence of our whole class. We were not by any means brought up well, didn't know our p's and q's and refused moreover to speak properly or respectfully as soon as her back was turned.

Our concentrated looks centered on her totally. We followed her every move, a fact which unnerved her briefly each morning as evidenced by her perspiration, followed by a swabbing of her face with a lace-trimmed hankie.

She shook her head at Francene Fuchigami, whose mother made her wear around her neck an amulet in a yellowed cotton pouch, which also contained a foul incense and herbs. The blessed omamori guaranteed the absence of both slippery vermin and casual friends. Francene and I competed for Mrs. V.'s favor, no matter how much we accepted her obvious but peculiar interest in the boys only. She favored them shamelessly, but bullied them at every opportunity.

We would bring Mrs. Vincente anthuriums, tangerines and sticky notes, "Dear Mrs. V., Your so nice. And your so pretty, too," with high hopes. Maybe she would like me then, ran the thread of wishful thinking. Winning her favor took all of my attention. I had to stay neat and clean and pretend to be a good girl, somebody who could "make nice-nice" and "talk high maka-mak." To win Mrs. Vincente over, I saw that I would have to be able to speak properly, a complicated undertaking demanding control of all my body parts, including my eyes and hands, which wandered away when my mouth opened up. Therefore, in a compromise with my desire to shine, I decided to keep absolutely quiet, stand up with the stupid row and ignore the one I wanted to impress.

Mrs. Vincente was one of us, she claimed, because she herself had grown up in our "very neighborhood." Her school, too, she once let out, had been non-English Standard. We were surprised to hear her say that her family was related to the Kahanus, who owned the corner grocery store. We knew them, the ones who used to have money. She spoke, dressed and carried herself in a manner that was unlike any of the women I observed at home, but she fit right in with our other teachers who, like her, had gone to Normal School and shared her authoritative ways.

Difficult as she was, we could understand her preoccupation. Getting rid of ukus was a tedious job connected with beratings from your mother and lickings from your father. We always knew who carried ukus and were swift to leave that child alone. News traveled fast. All the same we could each remember what it felt like to be the "odd man out," which was the name of one of our favorite games.

To have ukus, to tell your close friends not to tell the others, and to have them keep the secret: that was the test of friendship. Like the garbage men who worked under the uku pau system, which meant that no gang or worker was finished until everybody on that truck helped the final guy unload his very last bag and everybody could quit, uku season wasn't over until every kid got rid of every last clinging egg.

At Christmas time Mrs. Vincente would wrap up a useful comb for each and every one of us. At the end of the year we would race each other to be the first of the crowd lined up at her massive desk.

We would each shyly request her autograph with the suggested correct phrases, "Please, Mrs. Vincente," and "Thank you, Teacha," so she must have been what we had grown to expect a teacher to be.

Because of Mrs. Vincente I wanted to become a teacher, wield power and know how to get my way. I wanted to be the one who would point out a minute, luminous silver egg sac stuck on a coarse black hair; shake it vigorously with arm held out far away from body, and declare victoriously, "Infestation . . . of . . . pediculosis!"

She would then turn to address the entire class. "This child must go directly to the nurse's office." She would speak firmly but in a softer tone to the kid. "Do not return until you can bring me the white clearance certificate signed by both of your parents."

Completely silent during class, I practiced those words at home while I played school. I turned to the class. I gave the warning to the kid. Mrs. Vincente was not to be taken lightly.

The day Joseph learned about ukus, I figured out teachers.

Facing him, Mrs. Vincente demanded to know the new boy's name from his own mouth.

"Joseph Kaleialoha Lee."

"Say ma'am."

"Hah?"

"You must say Joseph Kaleialoha Lee, ma'am."

"Joseph-Kaleialoha-Lee-ma'am."

"Hold out your hands, please."

Evidently he had not "paid attention," the biggest error of our collective class, one which we were to hear about incessantly. He had not watched her routine, which included a search for our hidden dirt. He held his hands palms up. I shuddered.

Mrs. Vincente studied Joseph with what we called the "stink eye," but he still didn't catch on. She must have considered his behavior insubordinate, because he did not seem retarded or neglected as he was wearing his new long, khaki pants and a freshly starched aloha shirt.

She reached into the big pocket of her apron and took out a fat wooden ruler. Our silence was audible. She stepped up a little nearer to Joseph, almost blocking out all the air and light around us so that her sharp features and steely voice cut through to reach our wobbly attention.

"What grade are you in now, young man?"

Joseph was silent as if in deep thought. Why wouldn't he say the answer? I nudged him quickly on his side with the hand nearest his body.

"Fot grade," he blurted in a small, panicky wheeze.

She turned on us all, enraged at our murmurs of anticipation. We knew for sure he would get it now.

Some girl giggled hysterically in a shrill whinny. "Heeng-heengheeng . . ." Probably Japanese.

"Quiet."

Business-like, she returned to Joseph with her full attention, peering into his ear. "Say th, th, th. Speak slowly." He heard the warning in her voice.

"Tha, tha, tha." Joseph rippled droplets of sweat.

"Th, th, th . . . everyone, say it all together: the tree!"

We practiced loudly with Joseph leading the chorus, relieved now to be part of the mass of voices.

"Say the tree, not da chree."

"The tree, not da chree."

"Fourth grade, not fot grade."

"Foth grade, not fot grade."

With a rapid searching movement which most of us missed, Mrs. Vincente swung around to face Darcy Ah Sing, whose hand was still stuck in her curly brown hair, scratching vigorously. Mrs. V. stared blackly into Darcy's tight curls with unshakable attention. In a matter of seconds, with an upward swoop of her palm, Teacha found the lice at the nape of the exposed neck and pronounced her memorable conclusion, ending with "by both of your parents," indicting Darcy's whole family into the crime.

"March yourself into the office, young lady." Mrs. Vincente wrung a hankie between her pudgy hands with tight motions. Head hanging, Darcy moved out wordlessly to the school nurse's station for the next inspection. We knew that she would be "shame" for a long time and stared at our bare feet in hopeless sympathy.

When we were allowed to sit at our desks (after practicing the "sks" sound for "desks": "sssk'sss, ssk,sss, dehss-kuss, dehss-kuss, dehss-kuss, not dessess, dessess, dessess") we were hooked into finishing our tasks of busywork and wearing our masks of obedience, totally subdued.

Then she read to us, as she explained that she would be "wont to do when the occasion arose," while we sat at our desks with our hands folded quietly as she had trained us. She enunciated each word clearly for our benefit, reminding us that by the time we graduated we would be speaking "proper English," and forgot the uku check for the day. Her words stuck like little pearly grains into the folds of my brain.

"The child . . . the school . . . the tree . . ." I could not hear the meaning of her words and scratched my head idly, but in secret. I yearned to master her knowledge, but dared not make myself the target of her next assault. I was not getting any smarter, but itchier by the minute and more eager to break free into the oasis of recess.

When the loud buzzer finally shattered the purring motor of her voice, we knew better than to whoop and scatter. We gathered our things formally and waited silently to be dismissed. If we "made noise" we would have to sit inside in agony, paying attention to the whole, endless, meaningless story, which sounded like all the ones before and wasted our precious time. Even Joseph caught on.

Once outside two teams of the bigger boys pulled at a heavy knotted rope from opposite ends. Joseph's bare toes dug into the dust right in back of Junior Boy, the tug-of-war captain. Clearly he wouldn't need any more of my prompting if Junior Boy had let him in. Beads of wetness sparkled off their bodies as the tight chain of grunting boys held fast under the bright sun.

Noisy clumps of kids skipped rope and kicked up the ground, twisting bodies and shining faces, all together in motion. Racing around the giant banyan, for no good reason, I scream-giggled, "Wheeeeeha-ha-hah!" Like a wild cat I roared up the trunk of the tree . . . just to see if I could.

While the girls played jacks, and the boys walked their stilts, we moved around groups trading milk bottle covers and marbles. We wondered aloud to each other. We spread the word.

"Ho, whatchoo tink?"

"Must be da teacha wen' catch ukus befo."

"Not . . ."

"*Not* not!"

"Yeah?"

"Ay, yeah. O how else she can spock 'em l'dat fast?"

That made me laugh, the thought of Mrs. V. picking through her careful topknot. She would have to moosh away the hibiscus to get in a finger. I mimed her by scratching through the hair I let hang down in front of my face. When I swept it back professionally with the palm of my hand, I threw in a cross-eyed, crazy look. Joseph pretended to "spock ukus" in my hair as he took on Mrs. V.'s exaggerated, ladylike manner to hold on to one of my ears like a handle and peer in to the endless puka.

"Ho, man," he proclaimed, "get so planny inside."

The recess bell rang, ending our sweet freedom. We pranced back to the classroom in a noisy herd. Teacha gave us the Look. We grew cautious. We would spend the next hour silently tracking Mrs. Vincente's poised head, while Joseph and I smiled knowingly at each other.

Eyes gleaming, Mrs. Vincente never disappointed any of us because she always stuck right on her lessons and never let up at all. She stayed mean as ever, right on top of the class. As for us, fourth grade ukus could appreciate the effort . . . so much not letting go.

In Answer to Their Questions

by Giovanna (Janet) Capone

*In this poem, an Italian-American explains
what* Italian *means to her. How does her
portrait of her community compare to
Rivera's portrait of his?*

Italian
is where I'm understood, loved, and included,
where aglio e olio
is Neapolitan
5   for soul food.

Italian
means my living habits
are not quirks
but ceremonies, mostly invisible
10   to the non-Italian eye.
My skin color is olive, not "white"
and the hair spreading down my arms and
     legs and over
the top of my lip
is a dense garden
15   cultivated for centuries
by Neapolitan peasants
digging, dropping their sweat
into the soil
like seeds, passing down their genes
20   breaking their backs to subsist
resisting their own extinction

down there nel mezzogiorno,
the land of the forgotten,
they clung like cockroaches to life.

25 Italian
means the boat
from the boot-shaped country
the immigrants teeming like lentil beans
in New York Harbor
30 exhausted and sick, crammed in thick below
   the deck
shoved into steerage like cattle
they made a three-week passage
over icy water,
watched their dead family members heaved
   overboard
35 by authorities who altered passenger lists
removing Italian lives
like lint
from old clothing.

Italian
40 meant my Neapolitan grandparents
losing their families one by one
to hunger and disease
forced to leave
one by one, eldest sons
45 first in line for a boat
that would deliver them
to a land where the streets
are paved with silver and gold.

Italian
50 meant my grandfathers Dominic and Donato
supporting their wives and children
by sweeping the streets of New York

the custodians, but never the beneficiaries
of that wealth.

55   But Italian meant
you do what you must to survive
You keep your mouth shut
celebrate what you got
and be thankful
60   you're alive.

It meant one generation later
five kids draped on couch and chairs
t.v. blares, Sinatra sings while the phone
    rings.

Italian American
65   meant whole neighborhoods
laid out like a village in Naples:
Ambrosio, Iovino, Capone, Barone, Nardone,
    Cerbone,
Luisi, Marconi, Mastrianni, Bonavitacola,
"the Americans" living side by side
70   with "those ginzos straight off the boat."

Italian
meant Sunday morning sausage and meatballs
foaming in oil,
a pot of pasta water set to boil
75   and the hollow tap of a wooden spoon

Italian
meant the old men playing bocce ball
in Hartley Park,
Mr. Bonavitacola roasting peppers
80   in his backyard,
and every nose in the neighborhood
inhaling the aroma.

Italian
was the sound of my cousin Anthony's accordion
85   as he practiced upstairs
squeezing the air
into deep hums and festival sounds,
the accordion strapped to his back
the sun glinting off chrome and black keys,
90   a taste of the Festa de San Antonio all year
long.

Italian
meant the yellow patties of polenta
frying in a pan,
a pot full of escarole greens
95   and Ma spreading the lentil beans
on the kitchen table,
talking to me after a day at school
sorting the good from the bad,
the good from the bad
100 at the kitchen table.

Or my sister Lisa
sitting the kids down,
pouring salt crystals onto a plate on the
kitchen table,
telling us: "Here's the white people,"
105 & pouring pepper over them, "And here's the
black people,"
& pouring olive oil over them, "And here
come the Italians!"
and us squealing with laughter as the oil
bubbles slithered
and slid over the salt and pepper,
retaining their distinct
110 and voluptuous identity.

But Italian
also means those garlic breath bastards
dirty dago wops with greasy skin
ginzos straight off the boat
115 slick-haired, like vermin they bring disease

Italian
means the entire Mafia looking over my
    shoulder
whenever I cash a check.
"Capone? She's from Chicago!"
120 and their laughter
because they associate my Italianness
with a killer and hardened criminal.

But second generation Italian American
means I do what I must
125 to survive,
means I won't keep my mouth shut,
won't shrink to fit
someone else's definition of our lives.

Italian American
130 means my living habits
are cultural ceremonies, not quirks.
My skin color is olive
And the hair spreading down my arms and
    legs and over
the top of my lip
135 grows thicker and thicker
the more I resist,
the more I insist
on possessing
entirely who I am.

Acknowledgments

Continued from page ii

United Farm Workers of America, AFL–CIO: "The Plan of Delano" by Cesar E. Chavez. Originally printed in the April 10, 1966, edition of *El Malcriado*. Courtesy of United Farm Workers of America, AFL–CIO. For more information: P. O. Box 62, Keene, CA 93531, Tel: (805) 822–5571.

Harcourt Brace and Company: "The Whistle," from *A Curtain of Green and Other Stories* by Eudora Welty. Copyright 1938 and renewed © 1966 by Eudora Welty. Reprinted by permission of Harcourt Brace and Company.

Alfred A. Knopf, Inc.: "First Confession," from *Collected Stories* by Frank O'Connor. Copyright 1951 by Frank O'Connor. Reprinted by permission of Alfred A. Knopf, Inc., a division of Random House, Inc.

Marie Hara: "Fourth Grade Ukus (1952)" by Marie Hara, first appearing in *Bamboo Ridge: The Hawaii Writers' Quarterly*. Copyright © 1990 by Marie Hara. Reprinted by permission of Marie Hara, who wishes to thank the staff at The Bamboo Ridge Press.

Giovanna (Janet) Capone: "In Answer to Their Questions" by Giovanna (Janet) Capone. Previously published in *Unsettling America: An Anthology of Contemporary Multicultural Poetry*, edited by Maria Mazziotti Gillan and Jennifer Gillan, Viking Penguin, 1994. Reprinted by permission of the author.